# POETIC KISSES

## A NOVEL BY: TYEMEASE

PARKSIDE ENTERTAINMENT LLC

## Chapter 1

Cory came downstairs in his basketball shorts and flip flops without a shirt. He was in the comfort of his own home, which he just moved into a few months ago. Beside a few pieces of furniture, T.V., video games, and a sound system there wasn't much in there. Anyone outside of his circle would have thought that he wasn't finished moving in, but he was. That was him, he felt like he didn't need much. Plus it was an upgrade from the prison cell that he spent ten years of his life in.

At twenty-eight Cory was just getting on his feet, trying to get stable in life. Doing that stretch set him back significantly, in many aspects of his life especially mentally. The mental setback was the aspect that he wasn't really aware of. Him moving in that house was the second piece to the foundation that he was trying to build for himself. The first was getting a job which he did upon his release. While in prison he took a Heating, Ventilation, and Air Conditioning trade, came home and started working for an HVAC company. He has been working there for a little over a year now. His main goal was to stay out of prison, besides that he didn't have any specific aspirations. He just wanted to get himself together and enjoy life.

Cory went into the kitchen and poured himself a bowl of honeycombs cereal. Afterwards he went and sat in his lazy boy chair and turned on the T.V., Murray was on. "Ah, I don't feel like this shit right now," He said to himself. He was about to turn the T.V. until he saw a beautiful lady come on stage and the crowd started applauding. Murry met her with a hug as if he really knew her. He then led her to a seat.

Beautiful women always captured Cory's attention. If she wouldn't have come out he surely would have turned. "Let me see what this broad talking about," he said to himself before putting the remote control on the coffee table. He picked up his bowl of cereal, brought it close to his face then took a scoop while reading the title of the show on the lower left side of the screen.

"I cheated with twelve men, our baby might not be yours."

"That's crazy," Cory said chuckling in between munching. The lady on the show was standing at the screen pointing at the baby picture next to the supposed to be dad's comparing features trying to convince the crowd that the little girl is his. "That's fucked up," Cory said with a mouth full of cereal. He was shaking his head in disgust, feeling sorry for the little baby. She was sitting there all innocent without a clue in the world that she was being exploited. He knew that she wouldn't be happy with her mother when she eventually found out that she was a Murry baby. Then again judging off of how wretched her mom was, if she grew up to be anything like her she might be happy that she was on T.V..

"I'm a thousand percent sure Murry. I was faithful to him," the lady said with a heavy down south accent.

Murry brought out the guy who she was saying was the baby's father. The camera moved to his mother in the crowd, then back to him. He threw his hands up and the crowd began booing him. He went to the side by side pictures and began detesting all accusations that the baby was his. He was pointing at the baby's features talking about how she don't look anything like him. His mother got up, the camera turned to her. She was claiming the baby. She had been helping take care of her since she was born.

"Yeah that baby his," Cory said finishing off the last of his cereal. Against his better judgement he was convinced. He wasn't buying O girl sitting there trying to act like she was a good girl nicely dressed in her best for the Murry show. However, the baby did have a few similar features as dude, plus Cory believed in the mother's intuition. Dude mom was claiming the baby.

"Moms always right," he said before getting up to answer the door. Around the same time he was getting up the show had went to commercial.

"What's good bro," Cory said giving his friend a handshake before letting him in? You just came from work?"

"Something like that," Deron responded. He still had on his slacks, shoes, and button up shirt. He was a manager at Wells Fargo Bank. "You walking around here with ya shirt off like ya weight up."

"I aint lose much since I been home. The chicks still loving me."

Deron and Cory had been friends forever. They grew up down the street from one another. It was a time when Deron ran the streets with Cory but he was smart enough to quit before ever getting into trouble. Even though Deron ended up taking a different path in life they still remained good friends. When Cory was doing his time in prison Deron showed that he was a true friend by keeping in touch with him.

"Hold up man, you about to make me miss ma show." Cory rushed back in front of the T.V. just in the nick of time to hear Murry announce the results.

*"When it comes to one-year old Jacina Travis, Brain you are...."* Murry held it right there for a second to build suspense, then he dropped it hard on them. "Not the father!"

Cory held his fist to his mouth like he was shocked. "OOOOOHHHHHH SSHHIITTT, that's crazy. See that's what I'm talking about, bitches aint shit."

Deron was watching Cory get over excited about this T.V. show. He just shook his head in disbelief.

"She had me fooled, swearing up and down it was his. Talking about she a thousand percent sure it's his. I'm telling you bro, that's why when I start having kids I'm getting a DNA test on all of them. I don't care if she got five of ma kids, if she pregnant with six I want a DNA test for that little mothafucka too," Cory said joking causing Deron to start laugh a little.

"You bugging."

"Nah, for real though, I don't trust these chicks, they trifling. They be letting anybody hit, then be looking stupid when they stuck taking care of a baby by themselves. Bitch, you know that dude wasn't about shit when you let him skeet in you. Then when somebody like me come along they be wanting to settle down, Fuck outta here!"

"This is trash, you need to stop watching these shows," Deron suggested.

"I don't watch them how I used to. I did ma bid off of these shows. Murry, Jerry, Cheaters and a couple of them court shows. Them shows showed me that bitches aint shit and that mothafuckas be doing all type of low life shit. I couldn't see it before because I was in the mix, now I'm disgusted."

While Cory was locked up he had an epiphany. He realized that everything that he believed in was bullshit, trash, and that he needed to throw it out if he wanted to stay out of prison and live a better life. In prison he witnessed dudes constantly coming back to prison as if it was their second home. He came to despise everything about how he was living, the people he was around, everything. Now he always had something to say about something or somebody he knew who wasn't right. He called himself being hard on people because he felt they needed somebody to keep it real with them so they could get their shit together. If not get their shit together then just get a reality check. These was the same tactics he used to keep himself focused.

"Come on so I can take you to go get your car. I got other stuff to do," Deron said.

Deron pulled up to Camden auto in his White Infinity Q37. It was a car that suited his pay grade. Everything he had he worked hard for so he felt like it was only right that he treated himself to nice things. He wasn't trying to shine with the jewels or the big rims. His shining was more sophisticated and classier. When a female seen him she seen a man well put together. In many ways he inspired Cory. He was an example of someone from the hood that didn't get caught up. He worked hard, had swag, nice things and got the ladies. He lived better and had more than a lot of dudes they knew who that had been selling drugs for years. The only difference was that he worked, but he also played.

Cory got out of the car and went in the shop. While patiently waiting Deron zoomed in on this brown skin beauty going into the hair salon nearby. She was looking like his type so he cut his car off and made his way over there.

Cory backed his Camry out of the shop. He didn't see Deron in his car when he pulled alongside it. A couple minutes later while hooking the Bluetooth up in his car he looked up and seen Deron coming out of the hair salon with some lady. "Ma man," he said to himself admiring how Deron always bagged official women.

The lady had on a business skirt suit like she had a position at some prestigious law firm. Her clutch purse looked expensive even though it wasn't clear what kind it was. All her curves were in the right places. Their conversation was full of laughter. Deron walked her to her car and opened the door for her like a gentleman. He chatted her up a while before she began to pull out of her parking spot. They waved goodbye and before pulling off she held her thumb and picky up to her mouth and ear and said call me. Deron nodded his head yeah with a face that said definitely.

"You gotta stop thinking you me," Cory said through the window. He held his right hand at twelve O'clock on the steering wheel and leaned his left arm on the door. Deron had opened his car door, got in and they started conversing through the windows.

"Ya chicks don't be coming like that right there. All ya chicks be birds."

"You crazy as hell, I got some official ones too."

"Yeah right, if you say so," Deron said starting up his car.

Cory was the first to admit that he loved dealing with smuts. They were fun, there was no strings attached, he knew what he was getting into, and they knew not to expect anything.

Cory didn't get offended at anything Deron said, it was how they joked.

Deron rolled down his passenger window then said, "Talk to me when you step ya game up fam. Ha Ha!" He pulled off leaving Cory with a smirk on his face.

Being as though Deron had been in corporate America for a while he knew how to walk the walk and talk that talk. Turning his hood and sophistication on and off at will according to the circumstances. His profession also exposed him to a different type of woman than what Cory was used to. A more Elegant career driven kind of woman. Therefore he had better options than Cory.

## Chapter 2

Spence walked out of the business meeting wanting to do a backflip semi tuck, but that would have been too much. He couldn't show that he was that excited. He had to maintain his professionalism. He had just became a member of the board at L-Tech, which was an upgrade, especially in pay. As he walked through the parking garage towards his car two of L-Tech's employees that was walking his way both greeted him with smiles.

"Congratulations on the promotion Mr. Bass."

"Thank you," He responded shaking both of their hands. He kept it moving wondering how could they have known already. He didn't tell them. Before that moment he didn't even know if they knew that he existed. All the times they walked by him without speaking. Respect or kissing ass depending on how one saw it was just one of the perks that came with the position he just acquired. He pulled out his cellphone to make a call.

"Hello."

"Hey baby, did you get that box I had delivered?"

"Yes, I got it. It's beautiful. What's it for?"

"I want you to put it on. I made reservations for us at the Ocean Casino resort in Atlantic City. I'll be home soon."

Spence had set everything up for his lady in advance. He was well aware of the promotion he had just received. At times he felt like he had been passed up because the color of his skin. Still he worked relentlessly for years, incrementally climbing the corporate ladder. At times his dedication to his career took a toll on his relationship with his lady. Even so she stuck it out with him. That caused him to love her even more. Tonight he wanted to let her know just how much he appreciated her.

**** 

Spence opened the door for his lady who was wearing a black dress that came an inch above her knee. It was really elegant, perfect for the occasion. He held her hand as she stepped out of the car.

"You look amazing," Spence said admiring her in the Mejor Lewis dress that he picked out. She wore it so well that he even was shocked at his taste.

"Thank you," Malia said blushing. "This is a nice dress."

She wrapped her arm around his. He gave the valet his car keys and they proceeded to enter the restaurant.

"Reservations for Mr. and Mrs. Bass," Spence said speaking to the lady who was at the desk.

Even though Malia wasn't officially Mrs. Bass, when doing such things Spence always made sure she was addressed as such. Letting her know that official or unofficial at the moment the tittle would eventually be hers.

The lady at the desk looked at the names on her list then said, "Sure, right this way." They followed as she lead them to a cozy table next to this huge window that took the place of a wall. It overlooked a beautiful lake. While seated Malia took a moment to enjoy the view. The lights were dim throughout the restaurant. The music played softly over the light chatter that came from the people who were pleasantly enjoying themselves. Not only did Spence feel like he reserved the perfect table, but he felt that the Chop House was the perfect place. It was an upscale spot with a natural romantic ambience.

The waitress greeted them with a smile, handed them a couple of menus and asked would they like anything to drink. They declined and the waitress said that she'll give them some time to look over their menus and that she'll be back in a split second.

"Would you like to order now," the waitress asked when she came back?

"Yes," Spence said and began reading off of his menu. "I would like the Grand Shellfish Platter and the Colossal Lump Crab Cocktail."

"Okay," the waitress said putting the order in the electronic device. "And you Mam?"

10

"I'll have the Main Lobster Cocktail and the Surf and Turf Entrée Salad. Also can I get this Red velvet cake and a bottle of Belaire."

"Okay, will that be all?"

The waitress collected the menus and headed towards the back.

"This is nice, I never been here before," Malia said scouring the room.

"I wanted this night to be special for us."

Malia could tell that Spence was feeling good. She could feel the positive energy radiating off of him.

"So I assume the meeting went well?"

"Better than that, I got a promotion."

"That's great baby, I'm so happy for you."

"I finally got my just due, I'm definitely feeling good."

"I can tell."

While they were conversing the waitress came back with a bottle of champagne followed by their meals. They toasted to Spence's promotion. Malia was genuinely happy for her man, but in her there was an empty void that distracted her, leaving her uncertain about the status of their relationship. She knew he loved her, even though he had his own way of showing it. However after four years of playing house she felt like love was all they had. There wasn't any kids or a legal commitment, that's what worried her the most. She came from a god-fearing Christian family where marriage was the standard, it was expected. According to her family traditions a relationship wasn't official until the couple was married.

Getting married was always Malia's goal in a relationship. She wasn't willing to have kids until then. Little did she know that Spence was about to give her the surprise of her life, but he was being apprehensive because he wanted the timing to be right. Even though he set this whole dinner date up for this moment he decided to hold off.

The valet pulled Spence's Grey BMW X5 around, handed him the keys and Spence set out for the Atlantic City express way. About an hour later the room at the Ocean Casino Resort they had checked in and was now walking the along the beach. Spence's open dress shirt flapped as the wind was lightly beating against the ting top he wore underneath it. As they walked the waves came washing in taking sand every time the water receded.

"It feels like I'm being pulled towards the water," Malia said as they walked the wet sands bare feet. She held her shoes with one hand and him with the other.

"Come on, let's go swimming," Spence said scooping her off her feet then moving quickly towards the water.

"No No," Malia said trying to kick out of his arms. She couldn't get out of his grasp, so instead of trying she wrapped her arms around his neck so she couldn't fall. "Don't drop me Spence, I don't want my dress to get wet."

"I got you baby," he said walking until the water was about knee high.

"You play too much. Look at your slacks all wet."

He looked down at himself but didn't care how wet his pants were. He was feeling good about life. While looking down he notice the ring poking through his pants pocket. He almost forgot that it was there. If he would have been thinking at the time he wouldn't have ran into the water and risk losing it.

"I wasn't going to let you go. I'm never going to let you go," he said letting her stand.

Malia looked him in the eyes wondering if he really meant what he just said. The sun was setting, the beach was clearing out. The board walk was still packed with people, but it was a nice distance away. In their language the Seagulls were rapping to the soundtrack of the ocean. Spence felt like mother nature had set the scene perfectly. They were still gazing into one another's souls when Spence dug in his pocket and pulled out a little black box. Right in the water he got on one knee and held the box up towards her.

After realizing what he was doing Malia covered her mouth in shock.

"Malia, would you bless me and make me the happiest man a live?"

Before he could finish Malia said, "yes" and began hugging him extra tight. Her eyes were felt with tears. She leaned on him so much with her hug that he went off balance causing him to sit in the water. It was a moment of joy for the both of them.

## Chapter 3

Kimberly awoke and glanced at her clock to see what time it was. She had to be to work within an hour. She glanced over at Gunz who was laying there sleep, mouth open with a string of dribble trickling down the side onto her pillow. A repulsive expression flashed across her face as she got out of bed. She went into the bathroom to get herself ready for work.

She didn't know how she had gotten stuck with this lame as she would tell her friends. She had only knew Gunz a few months, but he was already staying over her apartment every night like he lived there. It was her fault though. When she first met him he was driving a blue Yukon XL Denali. The truck alone was enough to hold her attention. She automatically assumed that he had money. Not legal money because she wouldn't give a square the time of day if he didn't own a watch. She was attracted to dope and coke boys. Being a drug dealer and having a nice car meant you was about something in the city of Camden. It was a symbol that you was doing something right as a hustler. Later Kimberly would find out that that's not always the case.

It didn't take long for Gunz to start smashing her on the regular. In the beginning she was feeling him. He was fly, the sex was good, and they enjoyed being together. Within weeks she opened up her world to him including her home. It didn't take long for her to realize what a mistake that was. It seem like every day she was finding something different that she didn't like about him. Especially when she had found out that the Yukon wasn't his but his manz Ru's truck. He actually had an old Malibu that he had registered in a fiend name. The illusion was gone and so was the attraction. Now she was looking for a way out.

After getting ready she woke Gunz up. He popped up with the stank face, looking like he had smoke a pack of cigarettes before he went to sleep.

"Huh," he asked looking like he didn't know where he was at wiping his mouth with his shirt. The slob was still visible on his sleeve. Kimberly didn't bother saying anything this time. It was like beating a dead horse. The first time it was acceptable but waking up every day next to a grown man that couldn't keep his saliva in his mouth and be having it all on her pillows was a major turn off for her.

"Come on, I need you to take me to work," Kimberly demanded while putting on her shoes.

Him taking her to work was about the only perk she got out of him being there. Other than that he was the only one benefitting. Free roof over his head, free pussy, free food, he took everything he could get. Not what she had in mind at all. She was looking for her life to be enhanced when they first met, not the other way around.

Gunz yawned, stretched, wiped the cold out of his eyes, got up with his hard on poking through his boxers and started to pursue her.

"Come here, let me get ma daily dosage."

Kim moved out of his grasp. "No, come on, you're going to make me late." She knew that he was going to want some, that's why she got dressed first and then woke him up so she wouldn't have to give him any.

"Better late than never, right," he said rubbing her butt?

"Don't do me like that Gunz. You're going to get me fired. We can have sex when I get off, I promise."

At first Gunz wasn't trying to hear it but once he seen how close it was to her having to go to work he cut her some slack. Kimberly was definitely relieved.

**** 

"Hey kim."

"Hey Faith."

"Girl why you looking so down?"

Kimberly didn't know it but what she was feeling on the inside was showing on the outside.

"I don't know, I'm just tired of dealing with this bum," Kimberly said referring to Gunz. "He draining me."

"What he be wanting to have sex all the time?"

"That's not it though, he dirty and broke. He's a burden."

Faith began laughing at the way Kim was saying it. She had formed her own opinion about Gunz just from the things Kim would come to work and tell her, but she never felt like it was her place to say anything until now.

"I never seen him but once you told me that his name was Gunz I knew he was weak. Aint no respectable dude going to name himself nothing whack like that."

"I know right, I should have known better. What grown man introduces himself as Gunz," Kim said. Yet she didn't think to question what kind of grown woman goes out with a man names Gunz. She didn't realize it but that said everything about her own standards.

"Why don't you just get rid of him?"

"It aint that easy, somehow he done moved in."

"Do he have keys?"

"No, but he always over."

"I got a remedy that'll get rid of any man," Faith suggested as if men were some type of unwanted pest. "Don't cook, clean, or give him any. I bet he'll leave then."

Kimberly laughed even though she knew Faith was serious.

"Either that or just tell him he gotta go, that you don't want to be with him anymore. I always find it easier to be straight forward."

"I rather do that because that other stuff is a little too extreme. I have to eat too."

"It all comes down to how bad you wonna stop dealing with him. Anyway, how he going to be in the streets selling drugs but living off of you? You not even supposed to be here working with me. Shit, you supposed to be living the good life, spending his ill-gotten means."

"If he had any," Kim responded.

"Well you moving backwards, because aint no way I'm working at no KFC and ma dude in the streets."

"Less talking more working ladies," their manager said while walking by.

## Chapter 4

Cory woke up in a cold sweat. He couldn't understand why he kept having this dream. He been having the same dream since he was young. To him it was a stupid dream, but it freaked him out a little because it was kind of weird. Growing up he watched a lot of scary movies so he wanted to contribute it to them, but it was something about it that felt symbolic.

Bad dreams couldn't ruin Cory's day though. Everyday outside of prison felt good. It was a bright sunny day in May. The weather was just really starting to change. The females were wearing short shorts and the dudes was bringing out their bikes (Motorcycles and Dirt Bikes). The city was live, that's why Cory couldn't stay out of it. It seem like everybody who moved out of Camden eventually came back. Even if it was just to play for a little. That's exactly why Cory came back, to play. He lived in Magnolia NJ, an outskirt of Camden. Wasn't much out there, it wasn't too many spots in South Jersey that had things going on. So he found himself in Camden in his natural habitat.

Cory pulled up to the Ivy Hill Apartments. As soon as he got out he heard his name being called. He looked up and waved at Eve. He knew that voice anywhere.

"Cory, come see me when you get the chance, I want to tell you something."

"Alright, I'll catch you later," he said walking by her second-floor apartment. His car was only parked a couple feet away so even though he wasn't beat he knew it would be hard to escape her on the way back.

He made his way to Chantel's apartment. When she opened the door she had on some black tights and a white t-shirt without any shoes. She was short brown skin with a fat ass that Cory began feeling on as soon as he got in.

"Where ya kids at," he asked?

"They outside somewhere," he responded.

Chantel's kids were only 10, 9, and 7. He couldn't understand how she would let her kids run the streets without knowing where they were. That really wasn't his concern though, at the moment he was just glad that they wasn't there.

"Let me get some of this good stuff," Cory said with her hugged up from the back kissing on her neck.

"You don't waste any time, do you?"

"I think I wasted too much time in my life. You feel how hard that thing is," He said pressing against her.

He began pulling her tights down. He bent her over the arm of the chair and began hitting it from the back. Her ass jingled in a wavy motion every time their bodies collided. Cory was balls deep when they heard a light knock at the door. It was her kids. It was no way that Cory was going to let them mess up his nut though. They had her kids waiting out there for another five minutes. When they finished Chantel pulled her pants up and went to the door. When she opened it her daughter zoomed by so fast that Chantel didn't even notice that she was crying.

"Mom, Tia peed on herself. She couldn't hold it," one of her sons said.

Cory came out of the bathroom just in time for the little girl to run in. Chantel followed her feeling bad.

"What's up Cory," Troy said happy to see him. Troy and Terrell are Chantel's son's. They were dealing with one another for a few months so the kids were used to him coming over. Cory was cool with the little ones, but he wasn't trying to play daddy. The two boy's father was dead. He had got murdered a few years back while Cory was locked up. The daughter's father was locked up somewhere. She didn't know him. Probably because he stay locked up. Any man that Chantel brought home was the man in their lives. She didn't shield her kids from them. They seen men come and go. Some they liked, some they didn't.

Cory stayed for about an hour chilling playing games with the boys. Before he was about to leave Chantel tried to hit him up for a couple of dollars.

"I'm fucked up," he said patting his pockets.

"Stop lying, you always got."

Cory made sure he was always good. That wasn't a question, his thing was that he aint giving nobody nothing. When he was in prison wasn't nobody sending him anything. He had to survive off of eighteen dollars a month after the state took out for his fines.

"I'm a nine to five dude, I'm always hurting. You out here messing with all these ballers. Tell them instead of throwing money at them strippers to let you hold something."

Chantel sucked her teeth and rolled her eyes. "I aint messing with anybody else."

Cory stood there smirking thinking how she must have thought he was stupid. He knew that she was a smut. Her mistake was thinking because he worked a regular job that he was a square, or that he didn't know what was going on in the streets. All the other dudes she was dealing with were drug dealers, getting tax free money. None of them treated her nice or had the same respect for her that he did. That's why it was harder for her to ask them for stuff.

"How much you need?"

"Four hundred."

"For what?"

"I'm trying to get my hair done."

"What," Cory said! *This bitch must have lost her rabbit ass mind,* he thought while laughing. Even though he wouldn't have given it to her. He would have at least understood if her kids needed something cause they needed a lot. Yet, she wanted to spend four hundred on hair.

"That's not a need, that's a want. Yeah, you going to have to get somebody else to help you out. I got bills."

He didn't really care that Chantel was disappointed. He was more disappointed that she would ask him something like that, and actually tell him the truth of why she wanted it.

While leaving he was hoping to avoid Eve, but she must have been waiting because she was standing over the balcony when he got back to his car.

"Cory, come here right quick," she urged. He tried not to show how pissed off he was as he walked pass his car up to her apartment. "You want to come in? I just got done cooking. I know she didn't feed you."

Eve knew her friend well. Chantel didn't like to cook. Most of what her and her kids ate came out of a box, can, or from a fast food restaurant.

"Nah, I'm good. I have to be somewhere."

"Well huh, let me make you a platter right quick," Eve insisted.

Cory didn't want to be ignorant so he followed her in. Eve was coco brown, 5'8, about 150 lbs., with curves in all the right spots. While making his food she kept bending over in front of him. Her nice round ass stretching them black tights until they revealed that she had nothing on underneath of them. She knew exactly what she was doing, and if Cory hadn't just gotten a nut off then maybe he would have indulged but at the moment the desire wasn't there.

"Here you go," she said giving him the platter. "You might fall in love with me once you eat that," she said giggling a little, secretly hoping it would happen.

She really liked Cory. She wished that she had gotten to him before Chantel did. She knew Chantel and in her mind she didn't deserve him. Neither did she according to the same reasons she thought Chantel didn't deserve him.

"I'm sure I will," he responded playing her little game. "You said you had something to tell me, right?"

"Oh yeah, about your girl. You know that she be creeping on you, right? With a few different dudes," Eve said with a grin on her face.

22

*These bitches are grimy as hell. It never seize to amaze me the things these chicks a do to get what they want,* Cory thought to himself.

It wasn't like she was telling him something he didn't already know. He had just met them a few months ago, and he was still a new face around after being gone for all them years but for her to think he didn't think that Chantel was fucking other dudes was like saying he didn't know the game. It was always naïve to think that the other person was naïve, but he didn't say anything.

The truth was Cory didn't trust no female. In his book they all were smuts given the right dude, situation, money involved, how comfortable they were or if they thought that nobody else would find out. To him they were freaks who thought they were slick and smarter than the average man. So while Eve was talking he just gave her a look like tell me something I don't know.

"She aint my girl. We're friends, just like we're friends. I don't have a problem coming to see you. Just give me a call," he said leaving.

## Chapter 5

Deron beeped his horn twice. He was in the middle of the street waiting for Ebony to come out. He had told her a head of time that he was on his way, to be ready. He sat there trying not to be irritated while wondering what was taking her so long. A car had turn down the street. He didn't want to hold it up so he pulled over, got out of his car and went to go knock on the door. After a few knocks she opened the door still trying to put on one of her earrings.

"Give me a moment, here I come." She left the door open. Went to grab her purse and came right back.

"You look beautiful."

"Thanks, you look nice yaself."

Ebony was dressed down from what she wore when they first met. That was her work clothes. Today was more casual, for the occasion. Even in her red and yellow sandals, blue khaki shorts and red and yellow t-shirt she looked amazing. She was one of them women who could bring the sun out on a cloudy day, which was what she must of have done because that day was one of the nicest days on record.

The date they were going on wasn't one of them regular eat and movie dates. They had been talking on the phone for weeks now, getting to know one another. Their busy schedules were always conflicting which made it hard for them to get together until now. Through their phone conversations Deron had found out that Ebony was going to school, majoring in political science while working on the upcoming Mayoral campaign. Her father was a real estate developer, and that he had been working on a building in Center City Philadelphia. Her mother was an accountant. The more he got to know her the more interested he became in her. She didn't come from the type of family he was used to growing up in Camden.

Deron and Ebony wasn't the conventional type of people. Just one of the many things they had in common. Since they did all that first date stuff over the phone they had decided to go somewhere exciting. Dorney Park Wild Water Kingdom was the destination they chose. It wasn't too kiddy for them. They both were hard working people who barely got a chance to enjoy themselves. The day was perfect for the amusement park. Ebony was sophisticated but not uptight. As soon as they got in Deron was able to see the little girl that was in her come out.

"Come on, let's get on that water ride," She said referring to this big slope that you had to lay on ya stomach and ride down on a board. Deron had let her lead the way. After that water ride they went to this one where they was sliding down in a donut looking tubes. They tried to do every water ride before moving on to the rest of the park. Afterwards they went to this little pool area where all the parents took their kids to play. Ebony had Deron taking pictures of her so she could later post on Facebook and Instagram. They also took some together.

"I had a lot of fun today Deron."

"Me too. It feels good to just get away and let go, don't it?"

"You don't know the half. I haven't let go like this in so long it's ridiculous. I can't wait for this election to be over. Between that and my studies, I be having so much to do."

"What's your goal in politics," Deron asked curiously?

"I want to do what I can to make the world a better place, starting with Camden. Maybe I'll run for Mayor, Governor, senator, or even president eventually."

"You got big goals, that's good though."

"Yup, they don't stop there either. That's why I work so hard."

Ebony was an all-around good person. She also did organized planning. She did things for the old folks as well as the youth to try to keep them out of trouble. She did fund raising for causes she believed in, and job fairs. Deron was amazed at some of the things she was into. He never met such an altruistic person. At times it was hard to believe that Camden could breed such a woman. It was said that nothing good comes out of Camden, but from the conversations Deron had with Ebony and things she told him that was going on in Camden that saying wasn't true. A lot of people was doing things and a lot of good things was taking place. The people saying that just wasn't in that world to see what was happening. They were too busy attracting the things that reflected their mindsets.

## Chapter 6

Kimberly, Shonna, and Isis were walking down south street browsing. They went in a couple of stores, but mainly they were window shopping, hanging out, trying to enjoy the scene seeing who they could catch. South Street was always packed with people from all over who went there to shop or go to the restaurants that was there, but it was also a social setting. There were a lot of spots there one could go to and have a few drinks and really enjoy themselves.

Lorenzo and Sons was the pizza shop Kimberly and her friends chose to get something to eat from. Not because it was something about their pizza that they had to have but because it was about ten motorcycles lined up with dudes standing around them smoking, eating, and trying talk to the ladies that were walking by. While walking in the pizza shop Kimberly had caught eyes with this brown skin guy with a big beard. She smiled with her eyes but kept it moving. Even with her back turned she could feel his eyes locked in on her. While standing in line her legs snapped back and spread almost in a bowlegged stance. Her thick legs draped from them short shorts enticing almost every man who walked by eyes to take a look. She knew exactly what she was doing. She had thrown the bate into the water now she was waiting for a bite.

Nell was on Kimberly from a mile away. Her walk was mean, and the way the sun hit them beautiful thick brown legs caught his attention like reflectors at night. Every step she took his way she became more attractive. All of a sudden what his friends were talking about didn't hold his attention anymore. She went in the pizza shop and he followed determined to introduce himself.

It didn't take much for Nell to bag Kimberly. In all actuality she bagged him. He was her catch for the day. She had a dude, but a chick like Kimberly is always looking for better. Not necessarily to do better, but to have better. Ideally a better man with more money. Naturally two of the dudes that Nell was with ended up talking to the ladies that were with Kimberly.

"Where ya'll from," Nell asked after getting Kimberly's name?

"Camden," she answered proudly.

"Camden huh," he said like he was a little disappointed.

"Why you say it like that?"

"Nothing, I aint mean anything by it. I got a few dudes out there."

Nell hit Kim with all the typical questions to show interest until he got her number, then he was trying to end the conversation so he could get her out of there and push up on the next pretty thing that walked by. Kimberly was totally unaware of this. She was too busy sizing him up in her own way. He looked good with jewels and a bike. She knew dudes with motorcycles usually had nice cars too. She looked forward to seeing what other kind of toys he had.

****

It was about 10:30pm when Kimberly walked through the door like she didn't have a worry in the world. If she didn't have to work in the morning she would have stayed out longer than that.

"Where was you at," Gunz asked?

"Where it look like?"

"You bring me back something," he asked trying to look through her bag?

She snatched it from him and said, "No, I aint bring you anything."

"Why you aint tell me you was going shopping?"

"I aint go shopping. I went to have a good time and happened to pick up a few things along the way. If you ever gave me some money maybe I'll be able to bring you something back. I need some money anyway so I can go grocery shopping," Kimberly said with her hand out.

Gunz sat back on the couch and said, "I gotta see what I can do."

Kimberly rolled her eyes then stepped off. She was tired of him. What kind of grown man didn't provide? "I hope you got somewhere else to eat then. You won't be eating up all ma food, not no more."

Their relationship was to the point that everything that they said to one another led to an argument. Lately all she did was talk filthy to him. That meant she no longer respected him, and when the respect is gone a female is going to say and do disrespectful things.

**\*\*\*\***

Friday night Kimberly and her friends went to Vera Bar and Grill in Cherry Hill. Kimberly's skirt accentuated every curve of her body clearly showing that she didn't have on any panties. Her heels made her ass sit up and look fatter than it actually was. Going out was her way of putting herself back on the market. She had slowed down a bit when she first started messing with Gunz, but now she was waiting for the perfect time to get rid of him. She didn't know if she still had feelings for him or that she was just used to having him around. Whatever the case she felt like she could do better.

Vera was packed with all walks of life in attendance. The outside patio was open and Kimberly and her friends were on deck. They weren't trying to dance, they just wanted to drink and socialize. They saw a few people they knew then it was the guys they were getting to know. The guys bought them drinks as they pursued the goal of trying lay them.

While the party was going on it seem like the folks on the other side were having more fun. Kimberly couldn't stop looking over there. She took another sip of her drink and her eyes went back to who it seemed like was the main attraction.

"You see dude keep staring at you," Isis asked?

"Who," Kimberly asked playing stupid?

"The light skin dude with the waves. He alright too."

"He need to come get at me then."

"He look a little timid, like he don't want to come over here around these dudes," Isis said prompting Kimberly to jump into action.

"You might be right. I'll be right back," Kimberly said stepping off looking his way hoping that he would see her. When her back was to him she really began wagging her tail.

O boy turned around and didn't see her where she was at before. It took a few seconds for him to spot her again. When he did he was on her heels. "Are you running from me?"

"No, I was making room for you. I saw you looking, but you act like you didn't want to come over."

"Don't try to act like you wasn't checking me out too," dude said jokingly. They both began to laugh. "Ma name Jav."

"Kim," She responded letting him know her name. You Spanish?"

"Ma dad Puerto Rican. Ma Spanish all chipped up though," he said smiling.

Within the first couple seconds of them talking Kimberly had decided that she was going to give him some. She was feeling him. From his swag to his personality. The feelings were mutual. From then on every drink was on him. A little while later she let her friends know that she was leaving with Him.

"Where ya'll going," Isis asked?

"Just to hang out," Kimberly responded.

"You just met him. Hold up, let me get his picture," she said pulling out her iPhone and snapping a few pics of them.

"Ya friend bugging," Jav turned to Kimberly saying. "Come on, I'm out."

"Make sure you bring my friend back. Call me Kim." Isis was always on a hundred, but when she drank she be on a million. Still she had the right ideal because Kimberly did just meet him.

Jav got them a room at the Staybridge Hotel. It wasn't too far from where they were. Kimberly haven't had her cat rubbed in a couple of weeks. That's how long she had been dodging Gunz sorry ass. She was hoping that Jav would handle it properly.

Jav opened the door and Kimberly stumbled in behind him. "You alright," he asked knowing how inebriated she was.

"Yeah, I'm good sexy man," She said walking up to him kissing him on his lips. She had backed him up to the bed while unbuckling his pants. His pants hit the floor and she dropped to her knees and began sucking him. While leaning back on his elbows he admired her tenacity. The suck was different when a woman was determined to get that nut out. The countdown was on for launch until she disrupted everything by getting up to take her clothes off.

Sucking dick had Kimberly's pussy extra wet. She had came from it, now she wanted to get hit from the back. She crawled on the bed and adjusted her face and arms around a pillow while keeping her arch in position. Jav got behind them cheeks, no condom, no thoughts of one. He just wanted to feel what them insides felt like.

At first Jav was the only one stroking as she moaned and told him how good it felt. Then she planted her palms and began matching his stroke, gliding back on his man while looking back at him. He had one hand on her left shoulder with the other on her right hip. Looking at her was driving him crazy, he began trying to get aggressive. He tried pulling her hair, but her wig came off. He was shocked. Knowing how women were about their weaves he was about to apologize but she didn't miss a beat. He looked at the wig and then the back of her head and became a little turned off. Kimberly took him out of his trance when she looked back and told him to keep going. He let the wig go and tried to pick up where he left off.

After they got it in they both felt like they just did a full body workout. Jav sat at the end of the bed and rolled a dutch of sour.

"Can I taste that" Kimberly asked?

Jav passed her the dutch after about four pulls. He couldn't help but to notice how different she looked from the club and now, Pre wig and post wig. It was like two totally different people. At the club she was looking top notch, make up on, eye lashes done, one of the baddest things in there. That's how she caught his eyes. Without her wig on she was looking like she had just had a fight on the Jerry Springer Show and got water thrown in her face and her wig snatched off.

That was on Jav's mind as they laid there watching T.V.. He chuckled a bit to himself at the thought. As the dutch got low Kimberly passed it to him and got out of bed and walked to the bathroom. She didn't even have to switch for that ass to bounce. Her ass had that uncontrollable bounce that be messing dudes heads up. Jav watched her walk and all that stuff he was thinking about a second ago was a distant memory. He adjusted his meat making sure he was ready to go another round when she came out of the bathroom.

## Chapter 7

Cory bench pressed the 315 for eight times, straining to get the last two up.

"Let's get it, come on, that's all you," E.J. urged in a fierce but encouraging way. He was standing over top of him ready to spot him if need be, but Cory had it. "Good money," E.J. said once Cory racked the weight.

E.J. was another one of Cory's friends. Big bulky light brown skin dude who look like he could be a defense of end for the Pittsburgh Steelers.

Cory got off the bench pumped. Everyone in there was checking them out. The men because of how much weight they were playing with. It's in man's nature to be competitive on all levels. The women were checking them out because they were the flyest in there. Some were overtly looking, others would hide their gazes but sneak a peek when they could. The attention they were getting had a few dudes in there feeling some kind of way. Mainly the dudes who walked around the gym like they were the biggest guys in the world. They spent their whole days in the gym trying to talk to the women and tell people how to work out with correct form. Whatever they was feeling they kept it to themselves, they didn't really want any problems.

Cory felt like he was back on yard time. He wasn't lying when he said that he didn't lose much. His back was still V-shape and his traps still looked like they had little monkey arms wrapped around them holding on for a piggyback ride.

Deron was slim and ripped up. His weight piece wasn't anywhere near E.J.'s or Cory's, yet it was getting right. When he was younger he used to be into sports but he only really started working out when Cory came home. He was seeing progress and the compliments from the ladies was something he was loving.

Deron sat on the bench and began moving his arms back and forth to stretch and soup himself up. "Let's go baby," he said to himself. "I don't do this for me. This for all the ladies. I'ma get this thing right for ya'll," he said and laid down positioning his hands on the bench.

"I should let this shit fall on ya neck," Cory said helping him get it off the rack. "Don't let me hear you say no sucka shit like that again." Deron had already taken the weight off the rack. When Cory said that he started laughing and struggled to press it back up. When he racked it they all began laughing. "For real though, I know I don't do this for no broads. I do this because I like the way I look and feel, just so happens the ladies like it too."

"See man, I could have done more if you didn't make me laugh."

"Don't blame me, you doing it for them broads. They're making you weak, not me. They be dudes down fall. Dudes be wasting a lot of time and money on these chicks and as soon as they get knocked every chick move right along to the next dude."

"You don't let up on em do you brah," E.J. asked?

"Not at all," Cory replied.

"Don't listen to that fool. He talk that now until some chick come along and have him eating out of the palm of her hands," Deron said.

"Never, I'm something like a pimp."

"You know pimps sell they own ass too," Deron said laughing.

"Well, I aint nothing like a pimp then. Fuck that, I aint going out like that," Cory said quickly switching it up. They all started laughing.

"Ya'll know Spence coming through tomorrow, right? He said that he got something for us," Deron said changing the subject.

"like what, a six figure job," E.J. said while sitting on the bench.

"Yeah right, he getting all that corporate money putting on for the man. The man aint stupid though, he know that fool really a thug," Cory joked.

"We're going to find out tomorrow. He want us to meet him downtown at the Victor. Everything on him," Deron said.

"Balling! That's what I'm talking about. I'm always down for a free meal," E.J. said. He was one of them big hungry dudes who could make the owner of a buffet tap out. He wasn't wondering what Spence was going to tell them, he was thinking about all the stuff he was going to order on Spence's expense.

**\*\*\*\***

Spence rode through the heart of Camden in his Audi RS 5 coupe. He turned the heads of many who wondered who was in such a nice car. He observed his city through his three hundred dollar Ray Band shades. It was just how he left it. A few new buildings downtown in the commercial area. It seem like for every new building they put up there was two to three more abandon houses. This wasn't a city that you could erect a few new buildings and call it revitalization. This was a city that needed to be knocked down and built back up brick by brick.

Spence was happy to have made it out of the hood. Born to a single mother, he was the oldest of six siblings. Four of them had different dads. Growing up he watched his mother go from one job to another in attempt to support their family, and from one relationship to another trying to find a good man. Some relationships were abusive, others were not the kind of men that any woman should bring around their kids. Spence had to become a man before he reached puberty. While other teens were playing in the streets he was working at Burger King making sandwiches bringing most of what he earned home to his mom to contribute to the bills. He definitely learned the true meaning of responsibility at an early age.

Spence loved his mother more than life itself. He took pleasure in helping her. Until this day he's still real close to his family. They always call big bro for any and everything. Seeing the struggles his mother went through, the sacrifices she made, not only made him appreciate her, but he learned to respect and appreciate all women.

"Look at this guy looking like Mike Larry," Cory joked.

Spence came through the door looking like a GQ magazine model, tailor made from top to bottom. All the ladies in the vicinity was checking him out. Since Spence was working in Atlantic City he had moved to Egg Harbor, a town nearby Atlantic City. He only got to see his boys every month or two. They all greeted Spence happy to see him. It was always something new when they got a chance to catch up.

"Yo, did you ever get that promotion," E.J. asked? E.J. was another one of their close friends. Real laid back dude. All he did was smoke weed, work, and play video games. His job involved something with gaming. He made a decent living off of it. It was the perfect job for him. He was doing something he loved.

"Yeah, what ever happened with that," Deron added.

"That's one of the things I wanted to tell ya'll."

"What's the other," E.J. asked?

"I'm getting married," Spence said with a big smile on his face. He knew that his manz would be the happiest for him and they were. They were congratulating him, slapping fives, and bigging him up on his accomplishments. They all knew that he was a good dude and how hard he worked to get where he was in life. Lord knows it wasn't easy. They were his closest friends from childhood. Deron, and E.J. knew his goals, dreams, and aspirations. Cory had missed that part of their conversations when he was in prison. He congratulated Spence but he wasn't as happy for him as Deron, and E.J. was. He had much to say, but he didn't want to spoil the moment. Cory felt like love was a delusional emotion and by holding his tongue he was doing his manz a misjustice.  Spence is his manz, a true friend, so however he felt Cory just wanted to be a supportive friend.

"Let's toast to the good news," Deron suggested.

"I want you to be ma best man," Spence told Deron.

"That's what it is. What better man for the job," Deron responded jokingly.

"I want all of ya'll to be at my wedding though. I want to really do it up. Starting with my bachelor's party."

"Good thing you aint go soft on us and start talking about you don't want a bachelor party."

"what? I aint one of them dudes. I'ma get it all out, because once I commit I'm fully in," Spence said responding to Cory.

"You better because the next time we see you you're going to be handcuffed and shackled bent over with a red ball in ya mouth. She going to be fucking you."

Cory laughed harder at his joke than anybody else. No one really found it funny, definitely not Spence.

"What you mean by that," Spence asked?

"Nothing man," Cory said realizing that he shouldn't have said what he said. He took another gup of his drink hoping that Spence would let it go. The Apple Crown Royal had his tongue loose.

"Nah, what you talking about?"

"I'm saying, once you sign them papers and that ink dry up the tables are going to turn. She got you by the balls. She going to have a say so in shit she aint got no business sticking her nose in. She going to start making demands, commands, and complaining. You giving that bitch too much power. That's when they start tripping. If you start acting up remember she's intitled to half of all ya shit. Why when dudes become successful they volunteer to give a bitch half. You might as well give me half. Call it an investment. I got some shit I want to do, I'll give you half the profits. At least you won't feel bad about it if we don't come up. On the other hand you going to be fucked up when you got to give her half. You see what happened to Jordan and Tiger Woods. Them bitches be trying to break the bank. The more you make the more they take. Ya'll know I'm telling the truth."

Everyone was looking around like they didn't want any parts of that conversation. The only one to say something was Deron. "No we don't. I think you had too much to drink."

"Not nearly," Cory said and continued. "Think about it, anytime a female got money they act like they can't date a dude that's making less than them, or that got a regular gig. Forget about getting married, they aint dumb like dudes. They're only getting married if it's in their best interest."

"Don't be referring to my fiancé as no bitch," Spence said heated.

"I wasn't referring to her as a bitch, I was just saying."

"You fucked the whole vibe up. We're supposed to be celebrating but you get drunk and get on some bullshit with this jail house analogy of the world," E.J. said disappointed that their conversation had even took this turn.

"Fuck it man, the truth hurts. That's why don't nobody want to hear it. I'ma start keeping ma mouth shut from now on."

"You aint speaking the truth. You speaking ya truth. You bitter because Keisha shitted on you when you was doing ya bid," Deron said.

"I aint worried about her."

"Yes you are, you just in denial. Ever since you came home you sounding like a scorn dude that need love. You gotta let go brah."

"I been let go of her. That was a blessing in disguise. She wasn't about nothing. All that just open my eyes to how these chicks really are."

Keisha was Cory's lady before he got locked up. They had been messing with each other for years. They also had been living together. He loved Keisha, took care of her and confided in her. Even though she was six years older than him they were still young. She really knew how to take care of a man and he looked at their relationship like they were already married, like they were already a family, especially since he didn't have any other family. It was unusual to find a hood dude that loved their lady as much as Cory loved her. Later he found out that she seen him as just another dude. It was evident by how she just moved on when he needed her the most. He left her the house he had in her name, money, and a car. She was his lifeline when he was down, but he was hearing things she was doing that he didn't want to believe. Of course she was denying everything, lying. Eventually she had got pregnant by somebody else and left him without even sending a dear John letter. Ever since then he felt like why should he invest emotionally in someone that could be gone tomorrow. That's why he was so hard on females.

The conversation ended up getting heated between Cory and Spence. Spence didn't like his vibe or the words that was coming out of his mouth.

"If that's how you feel I don't even want you at ma wedding," Spence told him.

"I don't give a fuck. I'm a real one, I don't give a fuck about shit like that."

The situation blew up and almost led to a fist fight. They left on bad terms.

## Chapter 8

Kimberly got dressed in a fury. Gunz didn't come home last night and she knew that he wasn't going to be there to take her to work. She called him about five times and he didn't pick up not once. She wasn't worried about him not coming home, he was a street dude, she knew they didn't come home every night. She was more upset because she knew that he wouldn't be there in time to take her to work and he knew the time she had to be there. Especially with all the things she do for him, the least he could do was make sure that she got to work. She called her mother and within about fifteen minutes her mother was there.

"Thanks mom," Kimberly said getting in the car.

"What happened to that dead beat," Kimberly's mother asked? She didn't like Gunz. She knew he wasn't about anything.

"He didn't come home last night."

"What type of man doesn't come home at night?"

"I don't know, we not clicking anymore. I don't know how I keep ending up with these no good ass men. I know I can do better."

"Of course you can, but that's what you attract. When you usually attract something it's because of you."

"What do you mean," Kimberly asked her mom naively?

"It's called the laws of attraction sweetie. The energy you give off attracts. It has a lot to do with ya thoughts, but also the way you walk, talk, and dress attracts certain kind of people. You wonna wear all that tight skimpy stuff, you're going to attract guys that's attracted to that,"

"All guys are attracted to sex appeal."

"Sex appeal and dressing like a prostitute are two different things."

Kimberly sucked her teeth and said, "I don't be dressing like a prostitute."

Kimberly's Mom didn't agree with a lot of things she did, but for the sake of their relationship she kept her mouth shut. However in this case Kimberly was asking for her opinion. Never the one to sugar coat things she was going to tell her how it is.

"All guys like sexy women but a decent man, emphasis on decent man, wants a decent woman that he could take home to his mom, have kids with and give his last name too. I don't like how you dress half the time. Now if your mom don't approve how are you going to expect a guy's mom to approve."

"It's a different day mom, don't nobody wear loose clothes no more."

"Yes they do, all the women with good men do. Let me ask you a question. When was the last time you went out with a guy that actually had a job?" After waiting a few seconds and not getting a reply Kimberly's Mother continued. "You know what I call a man without a job," she pulsed like she was waiting for a response but she really wasn't then she continued. "A bum! You deal with guys that can't take care of themselves so how are they going to take care of you."

They finally arrived at Kimberly's job. Not knowing how their conversation turn into a lecture she hurried to get away from her mother before it got any deeper. The sad part was she knew that her mom was right. She was always right, that's what Kimberly hated. She liked to do things her own way, which while fun for her at the moment never turned out to be what she hoped for or really wanted. Always sending her to disappointment.

Later that day when Kim got home from work she received a collect call. It was Gunz, she accepted it.

"Hello."

"Kim, I caught a bullshit charge. I go to court tomorrow for a bail hearing. I need you to come to court for me."

"I gotta work tomorrow. I can't be missing anymore days."

"Call out or something."

"I can't, I already missed too many day. If I miss anymore I might get fired."

"It's a bail hearing. I need you to come bail me out. You got me or not?"

"With what, my looks?" I don't have any money to be bailing you out."

"Stop lying, you still got that income tax money, right? I'll pay you back."

Gunz knew Kimberly still had her income tax money. He had seen her bank statement. She had filed her taxes late so she got them back late. Usually she would have been spent her tax money but she was trying to save up for a car.

Kim exhaled, the conversation was draining her. It was unwanted pressure. It was always something with him. She regretted allowing herself to put up with him for this long.

"What's going to be your bail?"

"I don't know yet, it shouldn't be much. I got a couple hundred in the sock drawer. Put that with it, alright."

"Alright," she said in a low tune.

"I'ma call you tomorrow early to make sure you up and ready. I love you."

"Uhm Humm," Kim said and then hung up.

What Gunz was locked up for didn't even matter to Kimberly. She was so upset that she had to choose if she was going to spend her hard own money on bailing him out or getting the car she wanted and desperately needed. Especially now that he was locked up. He was her transportation.

She went to the sock drawer to see about this money he was talking about. She pulled out some money wrapped in a rubber band. After counting it there was only five hundred and seventy eight dollars. She sucked her teeth and sat the money on the bed. She held her head with her left hand pondering the situation.

*Why do he even sell drugs if he don't have any money*, she questioned herself not understanding being in the streets and being broke. *I got more money than him and I work. Don't let nobody bring you down,* she thought to herself. The next words that came to mind was that of her mother. *If you keep dealing with losers you're going to be one.* She didn't realize how right her mother was until now. Them words was exactly what she needed to make up her mind.

Gunz bail was 7,500 after 10%, which was out of Kimberly's price range, so she didn't have to let him down. He didn't give up though. He kept telling her to call here and there trying to get his manz to contribute to his bail. She halfheartedly did what he asked, but broke dudes hang with broke dudes so none of his so called friends came out of their pockets to help. Not even dude Ru who he was trapping for.

The next few days were all phone conversations. Besides him trying to get her to get in contact with somebody their phone conversations were dull. Now that the physical attraction was out of the way and the mental had to be worked on she was realizing that they didn't have anything in common. He couldn't mentally stimulate her. He couldn't even write a proper letter. She would wreck her brain trying to read his letters. The misspelled words and run on sentences was giving her headaches. She questioned why was she still holding him down.

Before Gunz got locked up Kimberly was emotionally disconnected from him. The more he wrote expressing his love for her the more her conscious was getting to her. She knew most of that stuff he was spitting was game because he wasn't coming like that when he was living with her. He sent her poems and handkerchiefs with drawings on it that he had somebody in the county do for him. Letters that looked like a little kid wrote them, with cartoon characters and hearts on the envelope. He was doing what every jail dude did when they got locked up. These things didn't make Kimberly feel special though. She had been with him for too long and knew him well, so while he was talking forever she was thinking never again.

Kimberly didn't want to keep leading him on anymore. Once he started asking for money for canteen she began falling back. She sent it the first few times and went to see him a few times but she was tired of it all. Their last visit she was at the booth impatiently waiting. The visit hall was empty. She began to wonder if the visits were canceled and nobody told her. Eventually this tall dark skin guy came in. He had a low cut with a big beard, broad but not bulky shoulders. He looked familiar to Kimberly but she couldn't place where she seen him at. He looked like he was somebody in the streets though. That in itself turned Kimberly on. She wanted to see who was coming to see him. They locked eyes and to her surprise he came right over her booth. This told her that either he was crazy or didn't give a fuck. Getting caught disrespecting with somebody's visit could cost one their life in jail, but O boy looked like he didn't have any worries. After he picked up the phone she picked hers up curious to hear what he had to say.

"What's good beautiful? I know we don't have much time before ya visit come so let me give you ma name and everything so you could get at me. You got something to write with?"

Kimberly didn't hesitate, she quickly dug in her purse pulling out her phone and put his name and county number in it. Afterwards he walked off going to a booth on the far side so her dude wouldn't expect anything. A couple minutes later Gunz came in followed by a few more dudes that was getting visits. At the same time a few civilians visitors came in. Not suspecting anything Gunz sat down picked up the phone happy to see Kimberly. That was the last time she visited him.

## Chapter 9

It was 6:25am on a Friday. Cory was getting ready for work. Eve was getting herself together so he could drop her off on his way to work. They had been getting it in for about a month now. It's been a couple of weeks since he had that argument with Spence. He was regretting it. Spence was a good dude, a true friend and he was a brother to him when he was down. That's hard to find. He didn't know when, how, or where to start but he knew that he had to make it up.

He dropped Eve off around the corner from her apartment. He was still messing with Chantel and didn't want her to find out about their little secret. Even though he didn't really care. He knew that it was only a matter of time before Chantel found out, but in the meantime he wanted to avoid the drama.

Being as though Friday was payday the guys came to work happier than usual. Most of their money was already spent in their minds on beer, liquor, women, bills, and whatever else vice they had. Cory went about his Fridays like any other day. The money wasn't enough to make him happy. It actually did the opposite. Especially when Uncle Sam took his share. Giving up 35% of something he worked so hard for wasn't sitting right with him, but so far he was sticking it out.

Cory and three of his colleagues got into the company van. They had to go replace a condenser in Maple Shade. His colleagues were two white guys and a black guy. The black guy was about five years older than him. The two white older guys had been working in that field for over twenty years. The black guy Jack, he worked about eight. They had been teaching Cory everything about the business. Cory didn't want to just work as an employee, he was always talking ownership. He wanted to learn every aspect, from how to fix and repair to how to run the company. Jack and Cory were real fly. They never hung out after work or anything, but they would talk about what they had going on, sports, ladies, their weekends and everything else men talked about.

"Jack man, what's up with them bunnies," Cory asked?

All Jacked messed with was white girls and he always told Cory these funny stories about his sex escapades.

"Nothing man, you know same old same old," Jack said with a 70's pimp type voice. "I got this one chick name Taylor. She nice young blood she nice. She trying to take me to meet the family but I don't know. They from Cape May, I heard they a little racist down there. I pop up with her they mess around and pass out they see their daughter with the black man."

They both began laughing as Jack continued.

"Her body crazy though, ass like Kim K's. I be having her twerking and everything. She know how to do all of that. I'm telling you young blood, you don't know what you're missing. You know ma motto, If it aint white it aint right. I don't even looked at black women no more. I don't got time for their bullshit. White girls fun. Plus black chicks don't want a dude like me. They want somebody that's going to disrespect them, get drunk, go clubbing, and sell drugs. I don't do any of that. I'm a HVAC worker. A straight square."

Cory was listening and laughing. "They aint all like that," he said to keep Jack going. He liked to jail off of Jack. Use him for entertainment how he use to do dudes when he was locked up. The faster the eight hours seem like they were going at work the better.

Cory's pass experiences had him hard on all females, but Jack was on another level. He was on some self-hatred stuff like Uncle Ruckus from the Boondocks. Cory bad thoughts was from how Keisha shitted on him, but he couldn't agree with everything jack was saying. Inside he knew that black women were just as precious as the air he was breathing.

"I aint never going back young blood," Jack continued. Them Kardashians made it popular for the white girls to have big butts now they all got them. Injections or not that don't even cross ma mind when I'm trying to get some. I'm going to see if my friend got a friend for you. Just go out with her, see how you like her."

"I'm cool with that, I like all women."

Cory had never dealt with a white women before. He didn't even like dealing with black professional women just because they wanted to be wined and dined and he felt like that took too much time and energy. That's why he usually stayed with the regular hood chicks. They liked you, they'll let you fuck. Straight to the point how he liked it. He didn't have a problem with a little talking on the phone or doing a couple pop ups. As long as he didn't have to put a lot of time, money, and effort into trying to get some he was good.

Every time Cory got paid he was disappointed. To a regular person being an HVAC technician was something, it's a career. People go to school to learn it as a trade. To Cory it was scraps. He always thought about what he could be making, like he always thought about how much fun he could be having if he was still in the streets. To him the square life was a struggle, and it was boring.

Cory went to the bank and made a withdrawal of a hundred dollars out of his account. That was the budget he gave himself for the week knowing that it wouldn't last because it never did. He went home, paid a few bills online, then felt like what's next. Usually he'll call a lady over or go chill with his boys, but since the argument with Spence he haven't seen much of them.

"Fuck that, I aint sitting around this mothafucka stuck like I'm in a cell or something, them days are over," he said to himself before getting up. He got in the shower, put on some fresh clothes and left.

Cory went to the lodge downtown. It was a nice little spot in the city that usually attracted more of an older crowd. Thirty five and up was the standard, but as Cory looked around he could tell that not everyone in there met that standard. *Maybe I'm just getting old*, he thought to himself.

It wasn't him. Over the years the crowd change. Older people still came but they acted different than the old crowd that use to come. They listened to hip hop and that drew a younger crowd. In turn more problems started occurring. These things Cory didn't know about because he was away.

When Cory first went in there he noticed a few funny looks but he knew dudes are always skeptical of a new face. The chicks were checking him out as well. He sat down and had a few drinks. The bar tender was this old head who he remembered from back in the back. Between serving the others she kept coming back over to talk to him, which he didn't mind because he didn't have anyone else to talk to.

While speaking to the bar tender a women came and sat on the stool next to him. Cory saw her through his peripheral vision but he kept his conversation a live with the bar tender until she had to go serve another drink. The woman was one of the ones Cory thought didn't quite hit that thirty five mark yet.

"Can I get a Turquoise Daiquiri with a lime wedge," the lady sitting next to Cory ordered when the bar tender came back. "You going to pay for that for me?"

Cory had just threw back a double shot of Remy and was in the middle of chasing it down with a corona when he heard the woman at the stool ask him that. With eyebrows raised he almost choked as he turned towards her looking at her like she had spoken a foreign language. "What," he said like he didn't hear her. The tone of his voice frightened her a little.

"Nothing, I was joking. You from around here?"

"Nah, I'm from North."

"What's ya name?"

"Cory."

She checked her mental rolodex, but she hadn't heard of him. Cory had been away for a while and he didn't come home and get back into the streets. She didn't know that though. Because of the way he looked and carried himself she thought that he was in the streets like every other dude in the city.

"My name is Tiera."

"What you doing when you leave here Tiera."

"I don't know, it depends."

"Depends on what?"

"Depends on if we leave together or not."

"Alright, well I know what you doing tonight."

Once Cory found out that she was game he didn't have a problem paying for the next few rounds. Especially cause he liked to get nice before he jumped in something.

Tiera was tipsy hanging on to Cory as they left the lodge. The only thing on his mind was where he was going to buy the condoms from. He opened the passenger door to help her in his car. She got in, but before he could close her door two mask men ran up on him with their guns out. Cory stepped back with his hands up letting them know that he wasn't trying to refuse the robbery. He wasn't scared, he just knew what it was.

One dude had the front of Cory's shirt gripped up with the gun to his face while he was up against the car. The other dude ran his pockets taking everything. All of this was happening fast. Cory had this big gun in his face but he wasn't paying attention to that. He was looking at Tiera. She had gotten out of his car, fixed her skirt and walked off regular not bothering to look back. It was obvious this was something she had done plenty of times.

Once the robbers ran off Cory felt himself breathing again. He touched his pockets and realized that they took his keys too.

"Fuck," he said mad at himself for getting caught slipping. He was angry, his ego was hurt. He wasn't in the streets anymore but he still had that pride. He felt like whoever they was that they were supposed to know better than to rob him. What he failed to realize was that nobody knew him anymore. Definitely not the younger generation. "I'm going to kill that bitch," he said out of anger.

Cory went back in the bar to make a call. Fifteen minutes later E.J. picked him up. He told E.J. about what happened and what he was going to do to whoever once he found out who they were. E.J. wasn't trying to hear any of what he was talking.

"Turn down here," Cory said trying to see who was amongst the crowd down the street.

"For what," E.J. responded?

"I want to see if that chick down there. I'ma break her up."

"You aint getting ma car shot up. You might as well chalk it up bro. It aint worth it. You only going to get yaself into a world of trouble."

E.J. was from the hood but he wasn't into the streets. He tried it when he was younger but figured out that it wasn't for him. It was too much that came with it. Too many people he knew were dying and he didn't want to be one of them. He didn't turn down the block like Cory wanted. Cory was furious.

"I aint Chalking shit up, fuck that. Somebody gone feel it. I'ma learn that bitch, she gone tell me who them mothafuckas were. Then I'm going to see them."

Cory kept going on and on. E.J. tried to calm him down, but he didn't succeed. After dropping him off E.J. called Deron. If anybody had a chance of calming him down he knew that it was Deron.

"What! He got robbed? What was he doing out there," Deron asked upset?

"I don't know. I just dropped him off at his house. He was talking crazy and you know how he is."

"Yeah, I know. I'ma talk to him."

Deron knew that once Cory set his mind to something how hard it was to get him out of that zone. He called him immediately. Cory didn't pick up. He tried two more times within the next hour, still no answer. What he didn't know was that Cory's phone had gotten taken too.

****

Cory was mad as the hulk, but he didn't want to act impulsively. It took every bit of his strength to control himself. He dwelled on the situation until his head began hurting. He fell asleep hoping to feel better when he woke up.

The next day he felt even worse. It wasn't only because of what had happened, but he began thinking about all the rest of the problems he had. He got his extra car keys, called a Lyft and went to get his car. Afterwards he went to T-Mobile and brought another phone. He went to his iCloud account and downloaded all of his information on to that phone. That only took minutes. Now his mind was on the get back.

As he rode through his old hood this familiar feeling came over him. Since being home he had been purposely avoiding his old friends and neighborhood. That way it would be easier for him to fight the temptation of getting back in the game. Now he was moving off of emotions, letting his anger get the best of him.

Cory pulled up to front street projects in North Camden. His manz had the projects on smash. There was a bunch of people out there, drug dealers, fiends, hood rats, and kids. This type of scene kept the old people away. It was a calm chaos. In a city like Camden that chaos can go from zero to a hundred real quick. Cory had got some curious stares from people wondering what he wanted. He walked to this apartment where it was few females sitting out in front. "Is Pettie in there," he asked?

A little girl around ten went in the house like she was going to go get him.

"No, why, whose asking," one of the chicks out front said being smart.

A few seconds later Pettie's Aunt showed up to the door with the little girl that ran inside.

"Cory," the lady said staring into his face trying to see if it was really him.

"Aunt Nessy," Cory responded.

"Dam boy, you grown now," She gave Cory a big hug. They stood there talking. The three chicks that was out there was checking Cory out. One of them was Pettie's younger cousin. As she looked at Cory her memory began coming back. The other girls figured that if he wanted Pettie then he must be somebody.

Pettie's Aunt invited Cory in to talk. She called Pettie to let him know that Cory was there waiting. Ten minutes later Pettie came. He made Cory feel like he was fresh out all over again. This was his first time seeing him, and he was excited to see his manz after all these years.

When they came out of the apartment Pettie introduced Cory to his dudes that was outside. Cory remembered a few of their parents and even some of them when they were young. Pettie began telling them stories about how they use to run together when they were younger. The things they use to do. Some of these things were things he had already been telling his boys over the years when Cory was away. That's how some of them knew him before they ever seen his face. All this talk of back in the days brought back memories, at the same time made Cory feel at home. Pettie and his dudes smoked more than a Chinese factory in Hong Kong.

"Nah, I'm good bro. I don't smoke no more," Cory told Pettie who was offering him the dutch.

"You sure? I'm trying to celebrate ma dude being home. I aint seen you in forever."

"Yeah, I'm sure."

"I never thought you'll stop smoking. You used to blow more than me. You still drink though, right?"

"Yeah."

Pettie told his manz to bring Cory something to drink. Cory ended up chilling with Pettie longer than he thought. A half pint of Henny lead to him smoking weed. Before he knew it he was fucked up in the passenger seat of his manz truck.

"So what's up with you bro? You been home for a minute, what made you come see me now?"

Cory sat in the passenger seat of the tinted up F-150. They was parked where Pettie could have a good view of his money being made. Every dollar that came through there was coming back to him.

"I need a strap. I got stuck up coming out of the bar last night."

"Yeah, what they get you for?"

A couple of dollars, but it's the principle."

Cory didn't want to tell him that he only got stuck up for sixty dollars. Pettie probably spent more than that a day on blunt wrappings.

"Did you see who it was?"

"Nah, they had on mask. That's why I'm going to find that chick. I'ma get her to tell me who the fuck they was."

"You don't have to do none of that. That's what I got all of these dudes for. They do whatever I want them to do. Real talk, I don't gotta get ma hands dirty at all. As long as I'm doing this shit you aint gotta get ya hands dirty either. Word up bro, you might as well come get this money with me. I aint got no problem breaking bread with you. I need somebody out here I can trust."

"You can't trust none of these dudes?"

"Nah, not like how I know I can trust you."

Cory sat there in a zone. His natural instincts wanted to get money with Pettie. He knew that he could make a lot of money real quick and wouldn't have to worry about working.

"I'm saying, whenever you ready brah. This money here for the taking. Come through tomorrow and I'ma get you that burner. You too fucked up right now. I don't want you to get jammed up."

Cory went home thinking about the proposition. He couldn't decide what he wanted to do, but what he did know was that he wanted that burner.

The next day Pettie had it for him, an all black P89. Cory was drawn to that gun how Smeagol from the Lord of The Rings was drawn to that ring. As he touched the gun he felt the power go from his palm to his arm, then throughout his body. If he was a cartoon character the glow would have been seen shooting through his body. This was reality, but the power he felt was definitely real. It's been a long time since he held a burner. The feeling brought back sentimental memories, some good some bad. Cory looked up from the burner at Pettie who was looking at him smiling.

"What," he asked?

"I'm checking you out."

As they chilled in the projects Pettie filled him in on what he was into over the years. The kind of money he was getting, his beefs, the status of their old friends, females, and how it was out there currently. He told him how his old girl Keisha was a wet head, with five baby daddy's who dudes be tricking off on. Cory didn't even care. For another dude it might have been a pleasure to know that the chick who shitted on him was doing bad. For him it triggered no emotions. He had turned all of them off when it came to her.

It's been a long time since Cory hung around the way. Watching all them traps come through only messed with his conscious. Plus Pettie was still in his ear trying to lure him in. His trappers brought him thousands of dollars and he sat their counting it in front of Cory's face purposely knowing he was tempting him. Cory was definitely tempted but deep down he remembered how dudes left him to rot just like Keisha did.

****

Things wasn't the same when Cory went back to work. He was tired and hung over. Plus his mind was still thinking about all that Pettie had put on the table. Him, Jack, and a couple of other guys went on an instillation call.

"I think I found somebody for you," Jack said. "A friend of mine, real good peoples. Her name Jenny."

"How she look," Cory asked? Cory had his usual conversations with Jack to help time on the clock go faster, but his mind wasn't there how it usually be. He secretly battled with the decision rather to get back in the game or not. His job wasn't bad. It was an honest day's work. It's just the pay wasn't allowing him to live the kind of life he wanted to live. He was seriously thinking about calling it quits.

"She beautiful, and she got that milky silky," Jack said using these old head phrases.

"What's that," Cory curiously asked?

"That white skin."

"You funny as hell," Cory said laughing.

"She got a nice butt too. She was one of them female soft ball players. You know most of they be holding. I'm not setting you up with just anybody. She a good girl. You want me to make it happen or what? I can set up a double date or give her your number. Let me know."

"I'll let you know by the end of the week. I got a lot on my mind right now."

The rest of the shift Jack told Cory stories about her and some other chicks. Every job had a guy like Jack. He was one of them guys that talked from clock in till clock out. He was actually smart and could touch on any subject. He had his reasons for his taste in women, but overall he brought good energy to work.

## Chapter 10

Deron pulled over, got out of his car and walked around to the passenger side to open the door for Ebony. They hugged and French kissed.

"Am I going to see you tomorrow," she asked?

"I don't see why not," Deron responded.

She pecked his lips one last time before walking towards her house. Deron got in his car feeling good. He was really feeling Ebony. She was everything he wanted in a woman. From her looks to her qualities. Almost everything about her was a plus. She had a son that Deron had yet to meet. She didn't want to bring a man around her son unless they planned on starting a future together. That was something Deron respected. Them morals was one of the things he liked about her.

When Deron got home from work he called Cory and finally got an answered.

"Yo bro, I been trying to get in touch with you for days. What's good?"

"I been working."

"Well look, I really need to talk to you. We have to get together to peace this stuff up between you and Spence. Ya'll bros, we been through too much to let something small come between us."

"He the one was tripping."

"Nah bro, you started it. Sometimes you have to keep ya opinions to yaself. He had a right to be upset. He invited us out to celebrate. He doing something that he think is going to bring him happiness. As his friend you're supposed to support that."

For a second Cory felt a little bad. "I guess you're right," he said in a humble tone. Then in the next breath with a smile he said, "but you know me, I aint letting up on these hoes or the suckas that be brown nosing them."

Deron shook his head in disbelief knowing his friend still had some growing up to do.

"Whatever happened to that nice little thing you met at the shop?"

"That's my peoples. We been going out."

"You hit yet?"

"Nah, not yet."

"Dam, it's been a couple of months," Cory said knowing that wasn't like his boy.

"I'm taking my time with this one. I'm just going to let it happen."

"Man, you supposed to test every chick from the door just to see if they like that."

"Nah man, she aint like that. You can't come at every female like that."

"You don't know how she is, you didn't even try her. You could be treating a hoe like a housewife. That's how dudes be getting tricked, I'm telling you."

"All chicks aint like the ones you deal with. Ya chicks think the way to keep a man is by fucking and sucking him good. That's because they don't have anything else to offer. They were taught wrong. Not her bro, she different. I enjoy her company. She be putting me on things I aint know nothing about and you know I'm a seasoned vet. Her personality is lit. We laugh, joke, and have fun together. It's different when you really vibe with a woman like that."

"Dam bro, it sound like you really simping. Go ahead I'm listening," Cory said laughing.

Deron continued paying his comments no mind. "She got a job, a nice car, and her own home. Not section 8 like ya chicks. She got her own, no debt, no nothing. She got a baby from when she was married, but she divorced now."

"How old is she?"

"29"

"You make it sound good."

"I'm telling you all females aint the same. You gotta know when you got something good."

"I'm not saying they're all the same, I just think you should come at them a certain way to see where they at."

"That's that back in the day mentality bro. When we was young and all we was trying to do was get our dicks wet. We did that though. When you was gone we had fun, chicks from all over. When you was behind the wall we was in college on campus doing us acting a donkey. Pool parties, Pajama parties, clubs, bars, you name it. You get tired after a while, and you start to want more than a nut. You start to see that it's about more than the physical. Nowadays I want a woman who can stimulate me mentally. Who I can joke with and have a fly conversation with."

"Tables flipped out here bro. I don't know if you noticed, but you can't be hitting anything nowadays. It's a lot of people who got that pack. You can't think about what these women are going to let you do to them. It's about you having standards for yaself. Who you dealing with says something about you, because they don't give a fuck. They out here fucking dope heads, coke heads, wet heads, pill heads, and drunks. All this is fiend shit. You want to fuck after them, what do that say about you?"

"When you up ya game you have to come different. You have to do things with class, have something to talk about with the ladies. Politics, businesses, community issues, something other than drugs, baby daddy drama and how they was going to fuck this and that chick up for whatever reason. All that shit is irrelevant in the real world. We're grown now, stop thinking like this is back in the day."

"I hear what you're saying but all bitches are the same to me."

"If you say so." After saying all that Deron gave up, he realized that It was no use.

**\*\*\*\***

That night Chantel stayed the night over Cory's house. They had a good night together but the next morning Cory woke up with a lot on his mind. He sat at the edge of the bed holding his head.

"What's wrong babe, are you okay?"

"Not really."

Cory began shaking his head ashamed to tell her. Then he looked up at her and said, "Truthfully, I been thinking about getting back in the game. I tried to push it out of my mind, but it's stuck there. I wasn't even thinking about that stuff until I got up with ma manz."

"Who you talking about?"

"Pettie, he from North."

"I heard about him. So are you going to do it?"

"I don't know. What do you think?"

"I think you should, I don't see why not. If you dealing with him you going to be getting money. He be having it."

"You would say that it's in ya best interest. You not going to be out there risking ya life or freedom. You going to be the first one in ma face with ya hand out though. You don't give a fuck about me." Cory shrugged her hands off of his shoulders, got up and left the room. He wasn't about to let another chick use him then shit on him.

Cory went downstairs, Chantel found him lying on the couch with an arm over his face. This was her first time seeing him like this so she knew that what he had on his mind was really bothering him. She sat on the couch and put her hand on his chest. He removed his hand from his face and looked at her. She didn't know it yet but his mind went from struggling with thoughts of getting back in the game to getting her out of his life.

"I didn't mean it like that Cory. I was...."

"Yes you did," he shot back cutting her off. I know how bitches are. All ya'll motives are selfish. How about you take ya funky ass out there and sell some drugs and bring me the money, or even get a job. You got it easy out this mothafucka. You don't know half of the shit hood dudes go through to stay alive and out of jail. You don't have nothing stopping you from being successful. No charges, none of that. All you have to do is go to school for some shit and get a job. Stop trying to fuck ya way to the top. It's not going to work, ya standards are too low."

"You got mental issues. You need help, because you're not going to be taking that shit out on me mothafucka. It aint ma fault you broke. You better stop crying, get off ya ass and do something about it." Chantel got up, went upstairs, got dressed then stormed out of the house.

"Don't bring ya stinking ass back, and you bet not had stole anything either," Cory shouted. After she slammed his door he got up and locked it. Then went upstairs where he had a left over dutch from yesterday. Ever since chilling with Pettie he began smoking weed again.


## Chapter 11

E.J. was getting ready for the gym when Monica came in the house. He looked at the clock then at her like he was waiting for an explanation but she looked at him and kept it moving without saying a word.

"Where you been at," E.J. demanded?

"Out," she responded with an attitude putting her purse on the dining room table. Afterwards she went straight upstairs not caring much about what he thought or had to say.

E.J. was beyond mad. Mad was last night when he was watching the clock seeing what time she was going to walk through the door. He fell asleep waiting. When he woke up and there was still no sign of her he knew that their relationship was over. He been seen it coming but being the kind of guy he was he wanted to patch things up, try to make things work. He did everything he could to try to rekindle the fire that they had in the beginning. From wine and dinning her to buying nice expensive things. Monica only took advantage of his kindness.

While riding to the gym E.J. weighed the pros and cons of her as his lady because he was tired of getting played. *Pros: Cute, Nice body, fat ass, I love her. Cons: Attitude problem, expensive, dress like a whore, don't get along with my mom, disrespectful, know she's cheating etc....* The cons out weighted the pros by far.

****

Cory walked in the gym dragging. Deron and E.J. was already in there working out.

"Look who decided to show up after all these days. You fell off bro," E.J. said joking but serious.

"You look bad, like a smoker. Come on, it's on you," Deron said getting off the bench and going around the other side so he could spot Cory. We have to pump you up before people start thinking you on that shit."

"I don't know what kind of drugs you talking about but I don't fuck around with no white shit so stop trying to play me."

Deron had a questionable look on his face playing with him. Then he decided to talk about something more serious. "Whatever happen to that situation."

"Nothing yet, but when I see that chick I'ma make her tell me who robbed me."

"Don't go looking for that shit. Nothing good is going to come out of that situation."

Cory knew that Deron was right, but he wasn't looking to be right. He wanted somebody to pay. The reason Cory didn't really want to talk to Deron after he had gotten robbed was because he didn't want to hear any positive encouraging speeches that was going to discourage him from whatever he was going to do.

A couple sets into their workout E.J. started venting about the things he was going through with his lady.

"That's why you throwing the weight around like you crazy," Deron said.

"I have to take it out on something because if I put my hands on her I'm going to prison. We all know I'm too pretty for that."

"She don't respect you bro," Cory said. "When women don't respect their dudes they do what they want and say what they want. You know how I am, if she would have told me that she was going to a party I would have told her to go get Shown T's hip hop ab video and have a party with that. She can dance and work her fat ass out."

Cory's joke brought a little light to E.J.'s situation. They all laughed but E.J. could only find it but so funny. He was the one getting played. He was the one that had to go home to this lying, cheating, conniving chick. After they left the gym Deron got in his car and left. Cory and E.J. stayed near their cars talking.

"Yo bro, I'm messed up. I don't know how to handle this. I need some advice before I do something stupid. She really testing my patience."

"You sure you want my advice," Cory asked a little surprised? He was curious to know why his advice out of all of their friends who got themselves together with females in their lives. Plus knowing how he was.

"You was talking some real shit, I need that right now."

"Alright look," Cory said trying to figure out a quick and easy way to give it to his manz. "Don't do anything dumb that's going to get you sent to prison. It won't be worth it. Real dudes don't bug over pussy, that's what suckas do. Pussy is prevalent remember that. You have to let her go bro. You aint stupid, you know she cheating. When a female life don't revolve around you something aint right. They need that attention. If she aint getting it from you best believe she getting it from somewhere else. It's as simple as that."

"She want to be a whore and be loved at the same time. It don't work like that. You gotta stop being a Teddy Bear to these chicks. You be wine and dining them, singing to them and shit. Yeah, you think I aint know," Cory said causing E.J. to laugh. "I know you be on ya Barry White Shit. You be putting in all that work doing all this extra stuff, going to the movies, waiting three four months to get some then a dude like me come a long and I'm able to hit the same day or that week, and override everything you doing. You'll still be on hold. She'll respect me more, I'm telling you. Them hoes say that they want one thing but then when they get it they don't appreciate it. That's cause that shit they be talking is just a fantasy, a fairytale that every woman was fed by the TV when they was young. They hold higher expectations for their fantasy dude than they do for themselves. They say they want a man with a six pack and a chest and their body looking a mess. They want somebody who's smart, with money, ambitious, good humor, good personality, spiritual, that love god, and know how to treat a woman and all of that. Yet they don't act how a woman is supposed to act. Their mouths say one thing but their actions say another thing. You gotta make sure that they deserving of it bro. That's all I be saying."

Everything Cory was saying was making sense to E.J.. He had been through his fair share of relationships. He always came out on the losing end. He was beginning to think something was wrong with him. He knew he was a good guy. Cory was helping him see that the only thing wrong with him was the females he chose to deal with.

"You right bro, this chick don't appreciate anything. I had got her this Chanel purse she wanted. This thing costed three stacks."

"What! Dam bro," Cory said laughing in disappointment. "I knew you was treating her good, but man. Why would you do that? She playing you bro. You don't get no chick nothing like that. All man, I'm hurt. She got a three thousand dollar purse with a bunch of dollar store shit in it. Do that make sense? Did she have any of that stuff before you met her?"

"Nah, not stuff that costed that much."

"See look, you upgraded her and she still don't appreciate it. If I was home I wouldn't have let you domesticate no hoe. She don't even look the part. Did ya mom meet her?"

"Yeah, they don't get along."

"That mother intuition is real. Ya mom old school she know when a chick aint good for her boy. She probably came in there dressed like a hooker and ya mom looking at her then at you thinking boy what's wrong with you bringing that girl in here. If mom don't approve she have to go, that's law."

"You saying all that but look at the females you be dealing with."

"I'm not trying to settle down though. I learned my lesson. I know the ones I deal with aint shit so I know how to treat them. They know they can't peel me for anything. We fuck and have fun, that's it. I'm all about being friends."

Cory knew for the most part that what he was saying to E.J. was going in one ear and out the other. A sucka was a sucka, friend or not. Cory treated females how they wanted to be treated. He let them be who they wanted to be and treated them accordingly. Not to many dudes was on it like that though. It was never hard for females to find suckas. He didn't really want to call his friend one so he just labeled him as a tender dick ass dude.

"You have to find a woman that fit ya status bro. You got yaself together, that's rare nowadays. You have to find a female that's about something. Believe me when I tell you, a female with herself together aint going to down grade for no man. They're too superficial. Especially the ones that got a little something, they all off this power couple stuff."

## Chapter 12

"Thank you for bringing me home mom."

"You ma baby. I don't have a problem coming to get you. What happened to your boyfriend car?"

"I don't know. I'm done with him."

"What happened?"

"He in jail, that's what happened. He can't do anything for me in there." When Kimberly decided to leave Gunz alone she also decided not to write the other dude she met at visit that day. "I'm about to change my number. He keep having people call me on the three way. I should have enough to get my own car now. At least make a down payment."

"How much do you have?"

"Thirty five hundred. You going to take me?"

"Of course, how else are you going to get there. You know you think you too good for public transportation."

Kimberly began laughing because her mother was right. She turned the TV on and The Steve Harvey Show was on. The Episode was about a woman that was attracted to bad boys. That caught Kim's attention.

"So, why do you think you are attracted to these so called bad boys," Steve asked?

"I don't know Steve. They got swag, plus their fun."

"So, What's the problem then? It seems like you be enjoying yourself."

"It starts out good, but then I can't get in touch with them when I want, they start being mean, I find out they're cheating. They don't want to commit. It's not how regular relationships are supposed to be, but for some reason I end up dating the same type of guys."

Steve stood in front of her with this sarcastic look on his face and said, "It's a reason why they're bad boys, they don't follow rules. Tell me, where do you usually meet these type of men?"

"Most of the time at the bar or at a club."

"There you go right there," Steve said and turned to the crowd in a teachers tone. "Ladies, when a guy goes to the club they're not looking for a woman to take home to their mother, they're looking for a woman that's been drinking enough to let them take them home that night."

Kim was sucking up everything Steve was saying. It made her think of the last time she was at a club, she ended up having sex with Jav and he never called her after that night.

"What kind of man are you looking for," Steve continued?

"I want a man that's tall, dark, handsome, with money, nice body, I love a cold six pack." She started giggling as Steve made faces. "I want him to be smart, morally sound, have integrity, and be spiritual because I'm Christian...."

She tried to keep going but Steve cut her off.

"You want the man of ya dreams, huh? Well what you want out of him you have to be. You want a man with his body right, then ladies have ya thing tight too. It work both ways. I'll tell you now, you aint going to find no man with money in any low budget bar. You have to go to Starbuck near wall street and catch the eye of one of them guys in them expensive suits. You have to go where the money makers are and dress accordingly. Like a lady, like you want to meet his mom."

Steve began talking about how he wrote about these things in his book. Plugging his book to the audience before he said, "I got these three guys here that I think would be everything you want and need in a man." Then he had the three guys brought out.

"I like this show, have you read any of his books," Kimberly's mom asked?

"No, but he was just talking some real stuff. I might have to buy them. He got me sitting here wondering why I keep ending up with losers."

"I can tell you why, because you keep dealing with them, that's why. All you deal with is street guys. Don't none of them have a business or a job. Them kind of guys don't care about themselves. Baby, you have to find someone that's going to love you. You have to choose a man by the way he live his life not his looks or what he has. That's superficial stuff. A lot of guys use superficial things to build themselves up to get women. You'll never find out who they truly are if you don't dig deep. You have to find a man that's confident enough to open his heart to you and love you. He can be kind and compassionate, yet stern and protective. That's why I been in love with your father for so long. He's a real man, he knows how to make me feel like a woman. That's how a man is supposed to make you feel. If he makes you feel less than that then he's not the one for you."

"I was thinking about that the other day when I had seen this white couple walking down the street holding hands. I felt a little jealous, I don't know why. It's like their men treat them like queens. I never had my hand held while walking down the street. Then when I was watching T.V. I saw this guy doing his wife's toe nails. It's like their men are so gentle with them and ours are so rough with us," Kim said.

"I understand what you're saying, but you have to deal with better guys maybe then you'll get some affection. Be a lady and raise your standards and expectations and you'll see a difference. When you meet this guy don't take his kindness for weakness."

Kimberly had a good mother and father that had raised her right. They wanted the best for her, but her expectations wasn't that high for herself. She was more into instant gratification. It took her this long to realize she wasn't getting what she deserved out of life.  That night she told herself that she was going to change the way she went about things, that she wasn't taking anything less than one hundred percent commitment from a man.

## Chapter 13

"Yo bro, what's good?"

"Who this?"

"It's Cory."

"Oh, what's up with you," Spence asked. He wasn't really mad at Cory how Cory thought. It was too much love and respect there. Spence just felt if he felt the way he felt then why should he be at his wedding.

"I wanted to call you to apologize bro. I was out of pocket that night. You know I got mad love for you. I support whatever you do bro."

"You ma manz, it wasn't really about anything. I appreciate the apology. I should be back in Camden not this weekend but next weekend.

"You busy right now," Cory asked?

"I'm about to leave for this meeting. I'm on the board of directors now, doing big things."

"I see. Alright, get with me when you get the chance."

Apologizing to Spence lifted a weight off of Cory's shoulders. He was thinking about it more than Spence was. Spence was too busy enjoying his success with his new fiancé.

As Cory was hanging up the phone Eve came strolling in the kitchen wearing his blue button up shirt. Cory was seated at the table, she sat on his lap.

"Good morning Cory. I was missing you when I woke up."

"I'm still here, he said.

Eve kissed him on the cheek. Cory, how do you describe our relationship?"

"Friends," he didn't hesitate to say.

"What if I wanted to be more than friends."

"I would say that's no surprise. Trust me, what we have a last a lot longer if we remain friends."

"Why don't you want a woman to take care of you?"

"Because I don't need a woman to take care of me. I'm not one of them dudes that need a female. I could get pussy whenever I want."

"Don't you want kids some day?"

"I'll have them when the time is right by a woman who knows how to play her part. She's going to understand me and know that I'm going to be me. Right now I'm good though."

"Don't you want to wake up every morning to this," Eve said moving her body on him?

"Every morning, nah. Whenever you want to chill or have a good time, maybe. You saying don't I want to wake up to you every morning like you the prize. You got it wrong baby, I'm the prize. Like Kanye said in that song, "It's a thousand you, it's only one of me."

Eve thought she had did enough to have him wrapped around her finger. She thought he was a good guy, she couldn't believe how he was talking. She didn't know that he was on all her moves from day one. From how she was telling him stuff about Chantel because she wanted him, to her trying to hook up on the regular knowing about the argument that him and Chantel had. She had told him everything that Chantel had said about him.

## Chapter 14

Ebony and her friend Asia had put together a charity event for the nonprofit girls organization they had together. The tickets were one hundred dollars. Deron was Ebony's guess which meant he didn't have to pay, but while they were standing there talking he presented her with a check for a thousand dollars. Telling her that he really believed in her cause. She smiled a beautiful smile then gave him a thousand dollar hug and peck on the lips. "Thank you," she said. Deron was still courting Ebony so that donation had multiple purposes.

Deron was impressed with the people she had at the event. There were Businesspeople, The Mayor, Council Men and Women, Lawyers, Judges, Teachers, and other professionals. It was a pretty elegant event. As they moved throughout the room Ebony held Deron's arm introducing him to everyone. Deron knew that she wouldn't be introducing him to all these prominent people if she wasn't feeling him.

They walked to their table and Ebony was greeted by a Beautiful Lady wearing a black dress. Deron noticed her unique style. Her hair was twisted in perfectly done dreads that wasn't locked. She wore what seem to him like afro centric jewelry. It wasn't much just a little matching ring, bracelet, and chain, all having the same color stones in them. She definitely made it look good. She also had a unique color to her skin. It was like a reddish to brown skin. Something like Native Americans, but she was African American. Her and Ebony greeted one another with a genuine sisterly hug.

"This is Deron whom I been telling you about," Ebony said with a smile happy to be showing him off.

Asia looked at them both as a proud sister. "It's about time I get the pleasure of meeting this brother. I been hearing so much about you."

"It's nice to meet you too," Deron responded softly shaking her hand. They chatted a little then Deron took a seat and Ebony and Asia went to the stage.

The event lasted a few hours. Deron stayed until the end to help Ebony and Asia clean up. Throughout the night he had two glasses of Pinot Grigio so he was nice nice. Ebony didn't drink at all because she was driving. She was a pure body, no smoking, drinking, snacks, or other foods that wasn't good for the body. Deron played the passenger side laid back.

"Did you enjoy yaself tonight," Ebony asked Deron?

"I had a good time. I met some interesting people."

"That's good to know. I was worried about you getting bored."

"Nah, I was chilling doing my own networking."

"I know, I seen you." Ebony liked the way Deron handled himself in there. She been realized that he wasn't the typical hood dude, but he still had that edge that said he was from the streets. That's what separated him from the squares in the corporate world. That edge was a major piece of him that she liked.

Deron was naturally Smoove and charismatic. His confidence showed in the way he treated others. That was another thing that Ebony liked about him. She was big on energy and his always seemed to be positive. Every time they talked it was always about something positive and progressive.

They arrived at Ebony's house. This was the first time that she invited him to her house.

"You live here by yaself," he asked admiring everything. The house was big and spacious. Pictures of her, her son, parents and other family members were throughout the house. Deron was thinking how she got everything, a good career, her own foundation, and own home. All she needed was a man in her life. He was hoping to fill that void.

"Just me and my little one."

"Where he at?"

"With my parents. It's just you and I tonight," she said seductively wrapping her arm around him.

"I like the sound of that. I hope that mean what I think it means."

"It means we got the house all to ours selves so we can have lots of fun."

Ebony tasted his wine coated tongue. Tingles shot down her spine as the intimacy began. Deron became excited but he knew that this was only first base. They shared kisses like these before. He was hoping that this was the day he made it to home base. Ebony seemed to have a lot of discipline when It came to abstaining from sex and he didn't want to seem thirsty as if all he wanted was that so he held her as they kissed waiting for her to make another move.

Ebony's breathing was heavy. She kicked her shoes off and pulled him to the coach where she took one shoulder strap down from her dress, then another. She didn't have on a bra. Her D-cups sat full and ready, nipples swollen. *Yeah, she ready*, Deron thought to himself. He helped her come out of the rest of her clothes. When they both were naked she sat on the couch and took him in her mouth and began sucking. He stood there looking down amazed that she actually knew what she was doing. For whatever reason he didn't think of her as a good dick suck, but he was glad it turned out to be so.

At first she was using two hands as she sucked and stroked him, then her right hand slid between her legs and she started playing with herself. The whole time moaning, licking, sucking, slurping, stroking, zoning out to her own rhythm.

Deron was at a loss for words, just looking down at all of this sexiness in motion. She didn't look up at him not once. She was focused, treating his meat like it was a delicacy. He didn't know where to put his hands. He didn't want to touch her head and mess up her motion. She didn't need any help or instructions. It was only so much of her head he could take before he was going to explode and he didn't want to do that without first feeling what she felt like on the inside.

He backed out of her mouth and told her to lean back on the couch. She defied his orders and got up wiping her mouth. You sit down, let me ride you. Deron felt obliged. As long as he was getting in them guts to him it didn't matter who was on top.

He sat down holding himself. She stood in front of him with her back towards him. She slowly sat on him and began bouncing, twerking, and riding. He pulled her hair from the back as they talked dirty to one another. She had her hand on his knees while plopping on him. He humped back from the bottom. He still had her hair as she bent all the way over to touch the floor while slowing her motion down. He began forcing the motion, making her ass go up and down. She began buckling. Legs hurting and tired she went to her knees. He followed her, still inside of her. While she was on all four he squatted over top of her from the back and kept stroking on an downward angle, using his thighs as a resting place for his forearms he held her by the waist pushing and pulling her back and forth. She was going crazy. The faster and harder he went the louder she got, loving it. Then right before he came he pulled out and let loose on her back. He stood up over top of her jerking off until he felt it was all out then he plopped back on the couch. Ebony stayed stuck in that position on the floor with her ass up. She couldn't move yet.

## Chapter 15

"I hope she alright," Cory said looking at Jack while he drove.

"I'm telling you man, she looks good. You're going to like her. She sweet too, a little too sweet. Total opposite of black women so don't do her dirty. I don't want to hear it about me hooking her up with a douchebag."

"You aint got to worry about that. Just don't give me a throw away."

"What you mean by that?"

"You know, the bunnies the white boys don't want because they don't look good enough for them. For some reason that's the kind I always see black dudes with. I never see them with like a Charlize Theron or Jennifer Aniston type. It's always a Miss Piggy unless he a star or a ball player. They be having some alright ones."

Jack began laughing because he knew what Cory was talking about. "You never dated a white woman before so I don't know ya taste. You don't even know ya taste. She nice man, believe me. Unless you racist and don't know it," Jack joked.

"Nah, I aint racist. I love women no matter what race. That's why I don't think I could ever be committed to one woman. They're like Ice Cream, they come in so many flavors. I gotta have some of all of them just because I like Ice cream."

"Well continuing with your ice Cream analogy, I'm not dealing with anything but vanilla from now on."

"Jack, what happened with you that you don't like black women no more?"

Jack made a face and took a quick glance at Cory almost to say how can you ask that. "What didn't happen," he said. "Everything stereotypical. Loud, miserable, angry, obnoxious, ghetto. I got tired of dealing with all the baggage from the previous relationships. Won't give me a heart attack. I don't have to worry about that with these Bunnies. They always got a good attitude, that's what make them fun."

"The one I got now when I come through that door she always hug and kiss me like she miss me. None of the black chicks I lived with was coming like that. Some aint even want to talk, no hey honey, or anything. I'm like dam, where's the love.

If I'm bringing home the beacon I expect to be treated like a king."

Cory didn't agree with what he was saying, he didn't disagree either. He wanted to understands Jack views that's why he asked lead on questions.

"You know I'm right," Jack continued. I went out with every flavor. You name it I had a scoop. I came to conclusion of what I like. They treat me good. If black chicks had a better attitude and treated their men better maybe they'll keep a man."

Jack was serious about every word he said. Cory spent the ride asking questions, picking his brain all while entertaining himself.

****

They arrived at The Cheesecake Factory. Jack's lady and her friend were already seated at the table waiting for them. Jack's lady stood up and greeted him with a big smile, hug, and kiss. Cory was checking her out, he could tell that it was genuine.

"Kathy, Jenny, this is Cory," Jack said introducing Cory. Cory shook both of their hands then turned his attention on Jenny. Jenny was impressed. She liked men with muscles, she could see Cory's poking out of his shirt.

Jack and Kathy carried the topic at the table since the other two didn't know each other yet. Cory asked Jenny side questions. He kept saying things that kept her laughing. He was charming her. She was feeling him. After the food was all gone, after the conversations had slowed up Jack looked at his watch and said, "It's late, I think we should get out of here. You ready," he turned to Kathy and asked? Kathy shook her head yeah, then looked at Jenny.

"You going to take my guy home," Jack asked Jenny?

."Sure, why not," Jenny answered.

Jack got up and did what gentlemen do, pulled his lady's chair out from under her then tucked it back under the table once she got up. Cory peeped his moves and the first thing that came to his mind was *I hope she don't expect that kind of treatment from me.* He felt that if she was going to like him then she was going to like him for being himself and pulling chairs out or opening car doors wasn't him.

As Jenny got up Cory's eyes scanned her body. *Dam, Jack wasn't lying when he said her body was right,* he thought to himself. In the parking lot she had a new Infiniti truck, QX80. Any wondering he had about what she did was answered during their conversation. He found out that she was a real estate agent. After finding that out he felt a little uneasy telling her what he did, but when he told her she seem not to judge him. He liked that, especially since he believed that when females be up that they don't be wanting to deal with someone with less than them.

"Would you like to go to my house and hang out a while longer," Jenny asked?

Cory didn't think twice about it. "Yeah, I don't mind." Now he knew for sure that she was feeling him.

Jenny lived in Woodcrest. A nice quiet suburban area. The only time Cory use to come through this town was on the train when he was young going to the Echelon Mall. He used to stare out of the train's window at the nice houses with the pools in the back yards and wonder what it would be like to live there.

"This is a nice house," Cory said looking around.

"Thanks, would you like something to drink?"

"Yeah."

Jenny came out with two glasses and a bottles of Pink Moscato. Cory had thought she was asking do he want some water or maybe orange juice. She sat next to him on the couch pouring them both some wine. As she handed him his class she held hers up for a toast.

"To a new friendship," she said.

"To a new friendship," he repeated.

Jenny was downing everything in her glass. Cory was sipping looking though his glass at her thinking *Dam, she must be thirsty.* They were already nice from the drinks they had at diner. After guzzling her drink she moved closer to Cory and kissed him. Cory got hard from the door and began kissing her back. She got on her knees and started unbuckling his pants. She pulled his pants down for him. Cory lifted the front of his shirt so he could see her go to work. The other hand he placed on top of her head as she began to slowly suck him.

It didn't take him long to rate her head game. One through ten it was about a five if that. He could tell that she liked doing it and actually thought she was good at it. She thought the sloppier it was the better she was doing it when it's not really about that. Her mouth was too loose, she needed to learn how to suck with the back of her throat. At the moment he wasn't willing to teach her, he just wanted to hit. He got her naked and admired her body. She was whiter than a Polar Bear, but hairless. He caressed her body, feeling on them pink nipples and areolas. He kissed her lips and neck then slid behind her. She got on the floor and bent over. Her pussy was pink as Alaskan Salmon fresh from the supermarket. That fat ass spread eagle excited him. He got in the pussy and started acting up, thinking about all the porn he seen when he was away. The Butt Man magazines and how rough them white girls liked it in there. He felt he had to try some of that stuff out on Jenny.

****

The next day Cory went to work and seen Jack. Once Jack saw him smile he knew that he had a good night with Jenny.

"What's going on with you," Cory asked?

"The question is what's going on with you. Didn't I tell you she was right?"

"Yeah, you was right. That you definitely did."

"What ya'll do when we left?"

"We went to her house."

"What, you got some, "Jack asked excited for him?

"Of course, I wouldn't be Cory if I didn't. She wit the shits, she let me do whatever I wanted and some stuff she wanted to do. I left her spot like five in the morning. I aint get no sleep yet."

"I could tell by how ya'll was at diner that she was feeling you. You should thank me for putting you up on a different flavor. You was going to grow old without getting any white pussy. I can't believe that" Jack said in disbelief causing Cory to start laughing.

They went on their assignments for the day. While they were at this one lady house installing a condenser Cory had told Jack that the lady kept checking him out.

"Who, me or you," Jack asked?

"Me man."

"Aye man, you attracting them bunnies now."

"I know right. You think I should push up?"

"Nah, you don't have to. They aggressive but in a different way. Watch she come at you."

"Are you guys thirsty," the lady asked with two glasses of cold orange juice in her hand not giving them an opportunity to deny it.

"Yes, thank you Ms. Caldwell. She gave one to the both of them and Jack thanked her as well.

"Your welcome."

They drank the orange juice like two thirsty camels. Ms. Caldwell stood there watching them, her eyes mainly on Cory. The t-shirt he wore was fitting him well revealing his muscles. He was sweating a bit so the shirt was sticking to him. Cory kept catching her checking him out. He was starting to feel how females feel when they knew dudes was looking at their bodies. He finished off the Orange Juice, gave her the glass and winked an eye. She smirked and blushed. He went back to work. She stayed with them talking.

Ms. Caldwell couldn't have been more than forty five years old. She was slim, average height with average looks. She started off talking about the condenser and ended up telling them about her divorce. Cory didn't miss a beat while working and asking her all the right questions to find out more about her. It was mainly the two of them talking. Jack worked while getting a couple of words in every now and then. When they were finished Ms. Caldwell walked them to the door.

"Mr. Allen," she said to Cory. She remembered their names from the introduction, plus their names were on their uniforms. When Cory turned around she gave him a piece of paper with her number on it. "Hope to hear from you soon," Ms. Caldwell stated.

Cory smiled and gave her a nod. "O you will," he said before stepping off. He got in the van and looked at Jack, "I'm about to change my name to The Bunny Slayer. It's about to get real," he joked.

"She pushed up," Jack asked?

Cory showed him the piece of paper so he wouldn't have to waste his breath answering his question.

"You know that saying, once you go black you never go back."

"I heard it before, "Cory responded.

"Well, I got my own saying. Once you start messing with them bunnies every day is Easter." Jake started laughing at his own joke. Cory didn't find it that funny, but he giggled anyway.

**Chapter 16**

Kimberly was riding in her New Blue Malibu. At least it was new to her. She had found someone selling their car on Facebook Marketplace. She got them to come down to her price range and was able to drive away. A new car and a new persona, now she felt like all she needed was a new job. Something better, she felt like KFC wasn't fitting her anymore. She became a regular viewer of the Steve Harvey Show. She was eating up every word he said. From watching his shows she became more aware of what men liked and wanted in a woman. She also became aware of the things she was doing wrong. Not only in her relationships, but in life. One of her favorite segments of his show was when he gave out tips on success.

Kimberly was beginning to not only raise her expectation and standards for men, but for herself as well. Her favorite quote from Steve was that "God wouldn't have created you and not have created your soulmate." Them words were like a revelation to her. They assured her that it was a good man out there for her.

She eventually found a new job as a 911 dispatcher. She had job experience but no particular qualifications. She felt like a dispatcher was better than where she was. It seemed like ever since she decided to change her outlook on life that everything started to fall in place for her. Her ex Gunz was still writing her wondering where the love was. At first the letters started out with him wondering why he wasn't hearing from her. Then he began trying to make her feel bad for not writing him, bringing up old memories, the times she said she'll always love him etc..... Then he would write blacking out on her, threating her, and cursing her out. It had gotten to a point that she wouldn't even read the letters, just trash them.

On the advice from her mother she decided to take a break from dating so she could focus more on herself. Kimberly pulled into the parking lot of Planet Fitness. Mind, body, and soul was her new motto. At 5'5 145 pounds, with a nice set of C-cups and a butt that some females get injections and die trying to get she didn't need too much of a workout. Other than just trying to stay in shape. She got out of the car wearing a pink halter top, some grey tights, and some pink and white Nikes. She grabbed her workout bag and water bottle and made her way to the gym. When Kimberly first started going to the gym she tried to convince a few friends to attend with her, but that turned out to be a waste of time. She had a better chance of putting a leash on a cat and walking it down the street. It just wasn't happening. Between her new job and activities she wasn't spending much time with old friends. Mainly because she started doing things they weren't interested in.

Ja'neece was a new friend Kimberly had met at work. She was the one who introduced her to the gym. Usually they'll work out together but this day Ja'neece couldn't make it so Kimberly was by herself. Ja'neece had showed her a bunch of different workouts and how to use the machines but since Kimberly was still kind of new to the whole gym experience she chose to stay on the treadmill and listen to music on her phone.

Kimberly was ten minutes into her power walk when she began turning it up and began jogging. Almost all the same people attended the gym. She would catch guys glancing her way, checking her butt out but none of them had the audacity to approach her. Even though she could tell that they wanted to. It was a couple of guys in there who she might have been willing to get to know, even though they weren't her type. Or the type of guys she was used to, but the type of guys she was used to wasn't doing much with theirs lives so she was looking forward to trying something different.

While she was thinking about the guys in the gym she seen this short cocky dude get on the treadmill to her left. She had slowed down and began power walking again. As much as she tried not to she ended up taking a look over their anyway. That was all he needed for her to think that she was feeling him. He smiled at her like a second grader saying cheese for his class photos. She smirked back but the after effect was bittersweet because she really wasn't beat. *O God, I hope he don't take that as he welcome to come talk to me,* Kimberly thought. He was the last person she wanted to talk to her. He was one of the guys she always caught checking her out, and every time she'll secretly hope that he wouldn't ever try to talk to her. She was into dudes who had their weight up but they were dudes from the hood who had swag and wasn't stiff. Dudes from the hood carried their muscles differently than squares. This dude was stiff as a board. Ja'neece had told her that he worked out at that gym seven days a week. Kimberly asked her how was that possible when it was only open five days a week, but that was the joke Ja'neece was making.

*Lord, I hope this muscle head don't try to talk to me,* Kimberly prayed during her power walk. The treadmill was facing the entrance. She seen three fine guys enter the gym. She had been inquired about them. Ja'neece filled her in on the little she knew about them, which was of their gym activities. They were like the only ones who Kimberly really seen herself giving some play to. Ja'neece had told her that they only came to the gym a couple times a week. This was probably her fourth time seeing them. While walking on the treadmill she purposely watched them workout hoping that the muscle head next to her would see that she was interested in them and not him.

\*\*\*\*

"It look like you got an admirer over there," Deron told Cory.

"Who," Cory asked after finishing off his Dumbbell Curls?

Not trying to be obvious, they all looked over there one at a time. They didn't want her knowing that they were talking about her.

"I think she looking at E.J.. He the one over here looking like the Rock."

E.J. started laughing. "She alright, and she got a stuffy. I might have to go see what's up with her."

"Remember what I told you," Cory said.

"What you tell ma boy? I hope not that garbage you be talking," Deron said.

"I told him when you meet a lady you treat her as a lady, and when you meet a hoe you leave her as a hoe. Stop trying to wife everything."

Deron gave Cory a funny look while he was talking. He knew that he was going to say something off the wall that he didn't agree with. "The last thing you want to do is get relationship advice from a dude that spent ten years jerking off. He love his hands more than any woman."

"You're right, joke on me. Joke won't be on me any more though. Either one of ya'll don't get more pussy than me now, and I aint going back to prison."

"I'm a committed man now, I'm past trying to rack up numbers. We still got ten years on you, so no matter what you playing catch up," Deron said.

"Wait, don't try to slide that in there like I wasn't going to catch it. You committed? When are we going to meet her," Cory asked?

"I might not ever introduce you to her after seeing how you came at Spence that day."

"Man, I was drunk. You know I got nothing but love and respect for ma boy. I called him and we talked about all that."

"I know, I'm messing with you. Eventually you will. I had just took her home to ma mom. She gave her the stamp of approval, now everything is a go. We taking it slow though. Told you she was married before."

While they were talking E.J. kept looking over at Kimberly to see if she was really checking him out. He wanted to go say something to her but muscle head dude had beat him to the punch. Before they left the gym E.J. looked back one last time catching Kimberly's eye. She didn't seem to be enjoying dude company. E.J. figured that he'll catch her another time.

## Chapter 17

Jenny had an open house for this house she was trying to sell in Woodcrest. It was a nice four bedrooms two bathrooms place. One of only three houses that sat in the Cul De Sac. The owner had rehabbed it himself and hired Jenny as his real estate agent.

Cory showed up wearing a navy blue blazer, some light blue jeans, and a pair of Air Force Ones. His hood version of being casual. Besides him there were three couples who showed up. Even though Cory was a guest he acted like he was viewing the house. He walked around with his hands in his pant pockets. He even ate some of the snacks and drank some of the free mimosas.

Jenny was in the kitchen telling a couple how the counter was marble granted. Cory admired her as she did her job. She was all business. She had her business dress suit on looking good. He slowly made his way over to her. When he got over there he began asking questions as if he had the funds to really purchase a home. Jenny answered each one like the professional she was without giving any hint that he was her guest. When everything was over Jenny escorted the couples out talking to them the whole way. She stepped outside to finish her presentation and then came back in.

Cory came out of the kitchen with a mimosas in hand. Jenny was locking the door. He was checking her out from the back thinking *dam, this bunny got it.* She turned around smiling. "You still here," she joked. She kicked her shoes off and walked right into his arms wrapping her arms around his neck and began kissing him. It kind of caught Cory off guard because she seemed a little too happy to see him. She backed him up to the kitchen counter. There he found a spot to sit his drink. "I couldn't wait for them people to leave so I could have you to myself," she said unbuckling his belt. She pulled off her panties, hiked up her skirt and lifted up her leg like a gymnastic gold medalist.

At first holding that leg up was nothing, but after a while his legs began shaking. He couldn't keep stroking and holding her weight. He decided to switch positions. He laid on the floor and she began riding him. Her double d's were bouncing around outside of her white button up shirt. She was going hard yelling like she was in a porno. Cory had both hands on her ass fucking back from the bottom.

After about fifteen minutes Jenny had got up, put her panties on, pulled down her skirt, and buttoned her shirt all while telling Cory how she got an appointment to show another house. She rushed up stairs to the bathroom then left. Her movements was kind of messing with Cory. She was nonchalant. She did her and kept it moving. Cory couldn't even remember her saying goodbye.

Even though they came from two different backgrounds Cory and Jenny had good chemistry. Their conversations were always good. They kept it basic but learned each other. They liked to laugh, joke and have fun. The sex was awesome and there was no strings attached. It was what Cory thought he wanted but if he didn't have to keep it real with anyone else he had to keep it real with himself. That's when he knew that he was starting to feel some type of way for Jenny. He fought them feelings with all his might. He knew it wasn't love, he felt that he wasn't capable of that anymore, but he did want to know her more than he did.

## Chapter 18

The sun began setting around eight O'clock. Cory was just pulling up to the projects out north. He had thought long and hard but came to the conclusion that he wasn't going back to the streets. It wasn't going to be easy to break this news because when certain things are in you it's like going against ones nature. He was trying to find the exact words to tell Pettie.

Disappointing Pettie wasn't the issue. He knew he had to do the right thing for himself.

Pettie was waiting on Cory. Whenever Pettie was around his goons were on alert. He stayed with beef and his boys were willing to pay the ultimate price to protect their boss.

Cory pulled his car right next to Pettie's truck.

"What's good with you," Pettie asked Cory as he got in the truck?

"You know, working, that's all," Cory responded in a low tone.

"Look like you was doing more than working," Pettie joked. "Why you got that stuff on ya face?"

"Oh shit," Cory said flipping down the sun visor to look at himself in the mirror. He began wiping the makeup off of his face. "I had just came from getting it in with ma bunny."

"Ya bunny?"

"Yeah, she official. About what we talked about though, I'm going to have to decline. I'm good bro," Cory said looking Pettie straight in the eyes to let him know that he was serious.


Pettie nodded his head slowly. Not in approval, just out of reaction. "I don't believe you when you say you good. I know you struggling with that little nine to five money. What you make ten to fifteen dollars an hour? Weed cost twenty dollars a dutch. A pint of henny cost more than that. I know you Cory, you going need more than that to live how you like to live."

*You used to know me,* Cory thought to himself. *One thing he is right about is that this nine to five bread is not doing it. I'm fucked up out here going from paycheck to paycheck. It's better than being in a cage though.*

"I brought that back for you too." Cory dug in his waist band and pulled out the gun Pettie had given him.

Pettie accepted the gun back realizing how much his friend really had changed. This wasn't the same gorilla that he remembered running up on dudes with the extendos.

"You sure about this? You don't have to be in the game to need one of these. You seen what happened to you at the bar."

"You right, but I'm good."

"I respect that bro. A lot of dudes are scared of change. They don't know how to be who they really want to be. Stay focused, if you need me for anything don't be shy to ask. You ma dude no matter what."

"I appreciate it bro," Cory responded. They got out of the truck and continued to talk. While standing on the corner a car slow rode up to the stop sign. The car was tinted but Cory could see that it was three dudes in there through the front. "Was that dude Ru in that car?"

"I couldn't see," Pettie responded. From his angle he couldn't see through the tint.

Cory was thinking about asking for that burner back. Ru was close friends with dude who Cory was locked up for killing back in the day. They caught eye contact for only a second but it was no doubt in Cory's mind that Ru knew who he was. Plus he probably been had heard that he was home.


## Chapter 19

*Vote Mayor Crumb for Mayor. Help take our streets back.* This was the slogan on all of the banners, fliers, and posters throughout the office building. There were plenty of smiles to go around. Everyone congratulating each other on a job well done with their victory. All of whom had put in countless hours trying to get people to vote for Mayor Crumb's reelection.

It was a victory party for all those who worked on the campaign. Ebony held Deron close happy to share in this moment with him. Before getting with Ebony Deron wasn't into politics but seeing how she lit up when talking about it interested him. She knew and understood it on a local and national level. At times she would break things down to him then go into history giving him an understanding of the world and why things were the way they were. He was humble enough to listen and ask questions and genuinely want to know. After some months he found out that her ex-husband hated when she talked about anything that he didn't know anything about, especially politics. Bout time she figured out how he was they had already had a kid together, so she felt obligated to work on what she considered minor issues at the time. Things never got better so she eventually decided to go her separate way.

There was a lot of commotion going on outside. Deron wondered what was going on. Then entered the man of the hour. A 6'5 light brown skin, bald headed brother with a big grey beard. This was the man who won the hearts of the city. Deron only met him once. He didn't know him personally but respected him to the fullest. Camden finally had someone in office who cared. Who really did good things for the city. He wasn't just a pond for the state how Mayors in the past had been. Mayor Crumb kept all the right people around him. People like Ebony who had organizations, who were doing things and contributing to the progress of the city.

Everyone applauded once he entered. He shook hands while making his way up front. The energy was electrifying. Mayor Crumb smile lit up the room causing Deron to smile as he applauded. For the first time he was proud of his city. For a second he felt ashamed that he never did anything for his city. Giving back wasn't a thought before. He had become complacent that he wasn't a statistic, one of the many who was either dead or in jail. This was a part of Camden he was just discovering. He wondered if any of his dudes would dig the kind of scene he was being exposed to. He kind of figured that out of all of them that Cory would be the least likely.

"Ya'll are such a cute couple," Asia said snapping Deron out of his thought. Mayor Crumb had just finished his political motivational speech. Deron and Ebony were still hugged up. Ebony had paid attention to every word. She really believed in the revitalization of Camden. Deron had never met a person so passionate about up lifting their city. Personally Deron didn't hear a word that was said. He was in his own thoughts.

"We're not only a cute couple we're perfect for one another don't you think," Ebony said hugging herself against his chest.

"Are ya'll going to the festival at the Ben Franklin Parkway tomorrow? Jill Scott and Marsha Ambrosius are performing," Asia asked?

"Them my girls. I'm going. Can you come with me baby," Ebony asked Deron?

"I might make it. Ma bro supposed to be coming in from Atlantic City. I barely get a chance to hook up with him how we used to. I already had plans on being with the fellas."

"Ya'll can come to the festival. Make that apart of ya'll day out," Ebony suggested in a pleading manner. "That way we could spend some time together, even if it's only for a little. I bet your friends would enjoy it."

Deron wished he could have spent every moment of the day with Ebony. That's how much he was into her, but he already had made plans to hang with the fellas so he didn't make her any promises. He did tell her that he'll see if the fellas wanted to go. If not he knew that there will be plenty of other times for them to share so he didn't sweat it.

## Chapter 20

Spence needed some time away from Malia. Ever since he proposed it seem like all she talked about was the wedding. They have yet to set a date but her and her friends were doing a lot of planning, making arrangements, online ordering a bunch of stuff, not calculating anything. The budget they agreed on couldn't have been a thought with the grand wedding she was planning. Spence wanted her dreams to come true but he was feeling pressure. His fear was that she was becoming a bridezilla. That would turn him off because that's the complete opposite of her personality.

****

"Who you say going to be performing," Cory asked Deron from the back seat?

"Jill Scott and the girls from Floetry," Deron answered knowing Cory had the least interest in seeing them.

"This thing bet not be whack."

"It's not going to be whack. This a grown folk event. These the kind of spots you find women who got themselves together at. If you lucky you might can bag one. I'ma tell you now don't go at them how you be going at them other chicks, you going to get played," Deron told Cory.

"I want to see you push up on something official, because how you be coming I don't got you down for dealing with women who be really on their A game. A woman who got themself together don't have to deal with ya shit so she not," Spence told Cory.

"They don't have to but they do," Cory responded back to Spence then continued. "I'm not going through this again. I'm going here to have a good time. I don't care what type of woman is here. I don't chase pussy, that's the difference between me and ya'll suckas."

"What's up with wifey, you still with her," Deron asked messing with Cory?

"Wifey who? You know I don't do that."

"Stop playing stupid. That hood booger that live in Ivy Hill."

"Chantel, I got rid of her."

"He back man handling himself," E.J. joked making everyone laugh except Cory.

"Look who's talking. Never need to do that again. I stay with a broad. I just moved on to her friend, and I got a couple of Bunnies on the team."

"You messing with her friend now," Spence asked? "You foul bro."

"How I'm foul? It's her friend, she the one foul. Females are supposed to hold themselves to a higher standard. Me, I could care less. I'm just fucking when I want. That's how it's supposed to be. You know how I feel about relationships. They don't count in the hood anyway."

"What you mean they don't count? I'm in the hood."

"Spence, you different. You got ya mind right. I'm talking about people with no morals or values talking about they want a committed relationship. They're not doing right by themselves, they can't do right by somebody else."

"That's one thing I agree with you with," Deron said.

"Ya'll be thinking I be on some other stuff. I know how things are, people are delusional. They let society standards tell them what's right like that's how everybody is supposed to be."

"For real Cory, I don't care how much sense you try to make I know what you been through. I know why you be on it how you be on it, but sometimes you have to forgive. You know they say forgiveness is setting a prisoner free and then discovering the prisoner was you."

"What am I holding myself prison from Spence?"

"Love, you need love bro."

"Love anything and your heart will be wronged and possibly broken. If you want to make sure of keeping it intact you must give it to no one, not even an animal."

"I give up. This dude is the Anti-Christ," Spence said throwing his hands up.

Cory started laughing. "Nah, that's a quote I memorized when I was down. It's true that's why it stuck with me."

Spence and E.J. was being entertained by their conversation. Deron wasn't, he drove seriously. Him and his dudes were like brothers, and he wanted the best for all of them. He knew Cory was smart, but he always been the most hood of them. Deron knew if only Cory would take that energy and applied it to something positive that he would be successful. He wanted him to realize that getting his life together was going to take more than stop selling drug. It was going to take for him to have a change in beliefs and attitude as well.

"You cutting yaself off from a major blessing of life. Besides us who you got," Deron asked rhetorically? "You don't got nobody else. You need a females love. A Companion, somebody to share life with, start a family with. I think you'll see life differently once you get that love."

"I get what you saying bro but we're at two different points in our lives right now. I just came home. I'm not trying to be lock down. Love to me is just a word of convenience that people use to manipulate the situation. I told myself I was never going to fall for that again. If I was to ever settle down, which I'm not, but if I was to she would have to be different. Not the kind that I'm used to dealing with, especially now that I'm done with the street life. She not going to have to go through any of the other stuff, doing bids and all that. I'm going to have to come up with a way to test her because I believe you never know if that love real or not if it aint tested. That's why them chicks fall off or prove to be disloyal when dudes get locked up. It was never real love. It was that bull shit hood shit."

****

The festival was packed. Free concert, everybody and their mom was out there. Cory understood what Deron was saying when he said this was a grown folks crowd, but this was a free concert that the city was throwing. It was an anybody crowd. It was mixed with all ages and races. About ten different artist were set to perform.

"Yeah, we just got here. We're over here where they sell the food. Right next to this ice cream spot," Deron said talking on the phone.

"Who this guy talking to," Cory asked about Deron. Him and E.J. was walking behind Spence and Deron. E.J. kept asking about the Bunnies Cory said he had. It intrigued him. Cory told him how he smashed Ms. Caldwell and how Jenny was a freak.

It was blazing hot out. All the people around was making it hotter. Cory took his shirt off and tossed it over his shoulder. He still had his ting top on. Him and E.J. went over to the dude that was selling waters. Cory could feel the ladies checking his weight piece out. He always tried not to get caught up in that because it always happened when he was out and took his shirt off. It made him self conscious. He wasn't a pretentious person.

While Cory and E.J. was talking a female made her way over to Cory trying to push up. She was light skin with some big titties but the only thing Cory could pay attention to was her hair. It was spiked up in the middle and shaved on the sides like a fashionable Mohawk. Her face was cute which probably gave her the confidence to get that hair style. While she was talking Cory cut her off.

"I'm sorry, you're not my type." He tried to say it as politely as possible but she still got offended.

"What mothafucka, you think you the shit? Fuck you!"

The ghetto came out of her. She wasn't even pronouncing words right while trying to curse him out. Cory walked away leaving her there feeling stupid.

"She started bugging out on you bro," E.J. said following him.

"That's why I walked off. Be real bro, I know I be dealing with some birds but they don't be coming like that. Where can we go together? Nowhere. I'll be fucking up ma swag dealing with her. What makes it worse she look like she was about forty trying to act like she was sixteen. She must of seen Rihanna do it and figured she could get it off. Not everyone could get that stuff off, she out here looking crazy."

E.J. was laughing making jokes as they walked back to where the ice cream was being sold. They saw Deron and Spence over there talking to two ladies.

"Spence aint ready for marriage, look at him," E.J. said joking.

"That look like that chick Deron bag that day he took me to go get my car. That's why he wanted to come here. He think he slick."

"Oh, that's the one he been bigging up," E.J. asked Cory?

"Yeah, that's her."

Jill Scott was on the stage performing. People were trying to get close to the stage. Cory was still paying attention to Deron talking to his lady when E.J. nudged him with his elbow.

"Yo, is that the chick from the gym," he asked?

Cory turned around squinting through the sun. "It look like her."

"That is her. I'm about to go push up," E.J. said amped up.

"Alright, I'm going over here with these dudes."

****

Kimberly was singing along with Jill Scott as her poetic vocals hypnotized the crowd. Jill Scott was performing all her throwback hits.

"Dam, this my song right here." Kimberly threw her hands up while swerving her hips. "I'm about to make a play list with all these hits on it," she told Ja'neece.

Kimberly like everything she heard from Jill Scott, even though she never really took the time out to appreciate it. Her live performance was touching her soul. She was connecting with every word. She was at a point in her life where she could finally understand what Jill was saying.

Being on this new vibe had Kimberly attending these kinds of events. Usually she would have hit a bar or a club, but her mom said something that stuck with her that she agreed with. She said, "she had to put herself in a position to find a better man." At first she didn't understand until she started hanging out with Ja'neece. She was going to places she wouldn't have thought of going before. Seeing how classy Ja'neece dressed made her change her style a little too. Eventually her mother took notice and began complimenting her, but it wasn't those compliments that she was giddy about. It was the different kind of men she was attracting. These men looked like something, smelt like something, they had a different approach. Never before had she been treated with such respect. She wanted to continue to hold herself up.

Her and Ja'neece had become real close friends. Going everywhere and doing everything together. She was spending less time with her other friends. She had become cool with Ja'neece's friends and family. Their friends were like night and day. The only thing they were the same at was that they liked to have fun, but what her friends were doing she did her whole life. Nothing ever changed, it was always the same bar and club seen. The things she was doing now was something new. It was always something different keeping her interested. It was just good vibes with her new crew, no shade or hidden hate.

"You really enjoying yaself, huh?" Kim heard a man in her ear say. She turned around kind of shocked that he caught her in the zone like that.

"Girl, why you aint tell me he was right there," she told Ja'neece blushing.

Ja'neece smiled, shrugged, and held her palms up like the emoji.

E.J. began charming Kimberly.

Meanwhile Cory made his way over to where his boys were. He knew that was the chick Deron had pushed up on the day he took him to get his car. He remembered because he was checking her out. She was looking good. On his way over a smiled flashed across his face because Deron looked like he was putting on. Cory noticed the unique beauty of the woman standing there with Deron's lady. They caught eye contact for a second or two before both looking away. He played nonchalant. It was going to take more than looks to amaze him.

"Where E.J. at," Spence asked Cory?

"He over there talking."

"Oh baby, this is another one of my boy's Cory. Cory, this is Ebony and her friend Asia."

"Nice to meet ya'll," Cory said.

The ladies spoke back and Ebony began pulling Deron arm trying to get him closer to the stage so she could see Jill Scott. "Come on, you know she's my favorite artist."

Cory watched as Deron's lady high jacked their day. He didn't know that they was going to be hanging out with Deron's lady and her friend. That wasn't part of the plan. Cory didn't say anything. They moved closer to the stage. Spence told them he'll be back. He went to go use one of the port a potties. Deron and Ebony was hugged up, enjoying the concert. Cory was seeing his manz at work. He held his arms around her as they both sang along. *Yeah, he in love,* Cory thought to himself.

Ebony's friend was standing there next to them by herself. Cory took it upon himself to go over there and keep her company. Asia looked up and gave Cory a little closed mouth smile. He returned it with one of his own. Asia wasn't shy, she was actually a confident woman, but reserved around people she didn't know.

Cory stood there talking to her. He wasn't trying to push up or anything. They talked about how their friends seemed so much in love and how it was a beautiful thing. Cory actually was in agreement. Not because Asia was a beauty that he might have a chance with. He heard how highly Deron spoke of Ebony, then to see them interact was witnessing the chemistry of love. Even though Cory wasn't at a place in his life to admit it he secretly admired that Deron had found love, that Spence was getting married, and E.J. was still on the hunt. He just wasn't there yet. He felt like he missed so much over the years that he deserved to be free. The vibe between Cory and Asia was chill. They were just talking and watching the people around them. Then Cory made a joke about Deron's head that had her laughing. Cory ended up enjoying the event more than he expected.

****

"So, how did you like Deron's friend," Ebony asked Asia?

"Which one?"

"The one that had the ting top on. The other one Deron told me is about get married."

"You talking about Cory."

"I see you remembered his name."

"He seem like a nice guy. We had a good conversation."

"Did he try to hit on you?"

"No, he was friendly. We had some laughs at ya'll expense. He didn't ask me anything personal. He probably has a woman."

"I'll find that out. If not, are you interested?"

"I don't know. He cute but seem a little rough around the edges. Not the kind of guys I usually go out with."

"I seen you checking him out a few times. Say you wasn't?"

"Who wasn't," Asia admitted! "I seen people checking him from afar. He knew it too, that's why I was trying not to be so obvious. Truthfully, I haven't stop thinking about him since."

"I'ma find out more about him for you," Ebony said while driving.

Ebony and Asia were tighter than most sisters. Even considering themselves sisters. They had been friends since elementary school. Both are beautiful, ambitious, highly educated women with a lot going for themselves. Ebony knew Asia better than anybody. She knew that she wanted a good man. She had high expectations, not only for herself but for any guy that she was going to deal with. Ebony commended her on that. She had high expectations as well. They strove hard to be the best they could be and felt they deserved the best.

Ebony was getting tired of catching herself not boasting or bragging but happily telling Asia about Deron and how good of a man he was. How he be doing this and that, taking her here and there. She knew her friend was probably tired of hearing about it too. Even though they were sisters and she was happy to see her happy, Ebony knew every woman coveted another woman that had a good relationship. Ebony wanted for her sister what she wanted for herself.

Asia would always tell Ebony that most black men can't handle a strong independent woman. That was her conclusion from the relationships she been in. She felt like after some men get to know her she either don't move as fast as they're use to their women moving, or they find out that they just can't tell her anything and have her head over hills for them.


## Chapter 21

Spence and his lady finally decided to set a date. May 24, they were hoping for perfect weather. Not too hot not too cold. He let his fiancé pick where it was going to be. It didn't really matter to him. Malia seemed fixated on all the details so he let her make all the arrangements. Unless she asked him for something he tried not to pay her any mind. He just shook his head yeah, but his focus was work. His new position demanded a lot of him.

His fiancé fell in love with this dress that she didn't quite fit. She purchased the dress anyway and started working out determined to lose about twenty pounds before her big day. Spence couldn't complain about that, he definitely noticed the extra pounds that she had put on over the years. Malia joined this workout club called Bridal Bootcamp. After she joined that she would come home drained not wanting to have sex. One day Spence decided to pop up on her to see what was really going on. Dude had the ladies working out doing all these crazy workouts, yelling at them like he was some kind of drill instructor. Spence looked into the faces of all the women there. Some were complaining, some lagging not doing it right, but when he looked at Malia she was going hard. He could see the determination in her. She had the look of an athlete that wanted to win. When she noticed him she smiled. He smiled back. Seeing how driven she was told him how much this wedding meant to her. It reassured him that everything was going to be worth it. Even though the prices of everything was ridiculous. The cake alone was $4500. Spence estimated that he would spend close to seventy five thousand if not more.

****

What! Almost seventy five thousand. You must really love her. I aint even know you was making that kind of money, let me hold something," Deron joked. "Is she contributing?"

"Nah, all me," Spence replied.

With a little laughter Deron shook his head at the thought.

"What you laughing for?"

"I'm thinking about what Cory would say."

"I don't want him knowing. I know he'll say something that'll make me punch him in the face."

"You don't have to worry about me saying anything. Now that I know when the wedding is I can take my day off in advance. Are you going to let the guys know or you want me to?"

"You can do it, I'm busy. Between work and Malia with this wedding I don't have time for anything. I be trying to stay at the office extra hours so I could relax."

"When is the bachelor party?"

"Like the week of the wedding. You're in charge of that."

"Alright, I got you. I already know what you like. Fat girls right," Deron joked rubbing his palms together?

"Come on man, don't do me like that."

"Nah, I got you. I won't let you down."


## Chapter 22

Kimberly answered the door like a seductress. With a big warm smile she greeted E.J..

"Hello little lady, you look spectacular."

"Thank you, you look nice yourself."

"I brought you something." E.J. brought his left hand from around his back revealing a bouquet of flowers.

Kimberly lit up, covering her mouth in awe. She gave him a big hug to show her appreciation. Afterwards she took her flowers in the house came back out and they went on their first date.

Bad Boys 2 had just came out. It was long overdue yet E.J. figured Kimberly would enjoy it. They both did, afterwards they decided that they ate too much junk at the movie theater to go to dinner. They chose to go over Philly to a nice little bar. It had an outside deck area where they sat, talked, and had a few drinks. Even though it was night out the street was lit up as though it was daytime. They were sitting there enjoying one another's company, talking about a range of topics from the movie they saw to getting to know one another to the muscle head dude that was in the way that day E.J. wanted to talk to her at the gym. She laughed When he described the help me face she had on when he walked by.

"Did you ever go out with that dude?"

"Sadly yes."

"Why you say sadly?"

"Because it was a disaster. All he kept talking about was working out, his muscles, what he do and don't eat, all this stuff I didn't want to hear. He was obsessed with himself. I think he talked about himself the whole date."

E.J. kept laughing at the way she was telling the story. He already had dude down for being the corny type. He always walked through the gym with his chest out, taking pride in his numbers, posting them on the board like all the rest of the muscle heads. Every conversation he had with somebody was how to lift a weight correctly. E.J. and his guys wasn't on that type of time. When they went to the gym they workout, talked, and laughed as usual.

## Chapter 23

"What do you think about us hooking Asia and Cory up," Ebony asked Deron?

They were lying in bed having their usual pillow talk. They weren't living together but Deron was staying over her house more and more. Deron had to take his time before answering this question. He wasn't sure because he knew how his manz was with women. When they were younger it would have been only right to bring his manz in with one of her friends but nowadays what his manz do could reflect on him and could possibly mess up the good thing he had going on. Especially since Ebony and Asia are so close.

"I don't know, Why?"

"I think she really likes him. Do he have a woman?"

"Wasn't they talking that day we was over Philly." Deron purposely dodged her question.

"They were, but he didn't try to talk to her on that level. He must have made a good impression on her. Don't tell him but she told me that she didn't stop thinking about him yet."

"For real?" Deron was a little excited. He knew he had to let Cory know this."

"I was kind of shocked myself. She's usually always in control. Is he single?"

Deron had thought he had dodge that question. He wasn't dealing with an idiot though, she came right back to it. Now he had to give her some kind of answer. "I don't know. I have to ask him."

"You know, how you don't know, that's your friend? Don't be trying to lie for him."

"Nah, I said that because one minute he is, the next he not. Half the times I don't know what be going on with him."

"Oh, if he one of them guys never mind then. I don't want my sister dealing with a guy with multiple women."

"He a good dude. Let me ask him his current status. I kind of believe he needs someone like Asia in his life. They probably would make a nice couple. I'll call him now, hand me the phone."

## Chapter 24

Cory walked through the house with the phone to his ear waiting for Jenny to pick up. The answer machine came on. He hung up then called right back. It took another five rings for Jenny to answer.

"Hello?"

"What's up with you, why it take you so long to answer the phone?"

"I just got in. I can't talk to you right now, I have company."

"Who you got over there that's more important than me," Cory asked half serious half joking?

"My man, I'll talk to you later," Jenny said before hanging up.

Cory stopped in his tracks for a second then started laughing to himself. He thought she was going to say her mom or a relative. He didn't know the whole time that she had a man. After hanging up he quickly got over what Jenny had told him and called Eve. He knew she'll be home no matter what time of the day it was. He preferred Jenny because she was a stone cold freak, but everything she did Eve did too.

"Hello," Eve answered the phone.

"You sleep," Cory asked?

"If I'm sleep how could I be talking to you?"

"You know what I mean. Get a Lyft so you can come over, I'll give you the money when you get here."

"Why don't you just come get me."

Cory agreed. He was trying to fuck tonight. He didn't have time to be playing. On his way out the house his phone started ringing. He looked at it and seen that it was Deron but he didn't answer it.

Instead of bringing Eve back to his pad he ended up smashing at her place. A couple of hours later he was going to his car when he seen another car slow rolling up. It was two something in the morning. All the windows on the car was tinted. Ivy Hill was flooded with hood rats. Cory knew whoever was behind that tint was either coming to scoop one up or dropping one off. It wasn't rare to see dudes creeping out there all hours of the night.

Chantel came out of her apartment. Cory laughed to himself. *I should have known*, he thought to himself. He backed out of his parking spot. She started looking at his car not liking that fact that she got caught creeping and wondering what was he doing out there at this time of night if he wasn't out there with her. Was he spying on her? He beeped the horn twice at her as he rode by. Her head followed his car all the way up the street.

\*\*\*\*

After a long night Cory still managed to make it to work on time.

"You look hung over," Jack said.

"I only got a few hours of sleep. I'm good though. Where we at today?"

"I'm about to get the schedule now."

The weather had changed. It was no longer hot out. Homeowners were now having problems with their furnaces. Today it was just him and Jack making runs. Once Jack came back with the schedule they was on the move.

"Why didn't you tell me Jenny had a man?"

"She got a man," Jack responded as if he didn't know? "She probably got back with her ex."

"You telling me to don't do anything to make you look bad, but she the one with a dude. She had me open for a little minute too, doing all this freak nasty stuff. I thought she was doing all that because she was feeling me."

Jack was laughing, he knew Jenny well. "All I told you was that she was fun. Was I right?"

"Definitely, but you had me thinking she wasn't like that. Then the vibe I was getting from her. She was all professional, I'm thinking she some other kind of chick. I aint going to lie, I'm not used to dealing with freaks who got their shit together."

"You have to understand just because a woman has a career doesn't mean they're not human. They got needs too. Them ones are some of the biggest freaks. They just carry themselves different."

Cory sat in the passenger seat listening. What Jack was saying made since. He still felt that he kind of misled him. He knew her so he felt that he should have told him exactly what he was getting into.

"Are you going to stop messing with her because she got a dude?"

"Not at all, if she fucking I'm fucking. I know I have to strap up now."

"I got some more friends like her I can introduce you to. They're just as cool. Getting it in to them is like going to go get ice cream. They don't deal with any complex. They be on it like we're friends why not have sex."

"Did you hit Jenny?"

"We had an episode some time ago. Nothing since."

"That's something you should have told me too," Cory said.

"I didn't think it was a big deal."

Cory had to remember that Jack was a different type of guy. A Square Pants Sponge Bob that didn't live by the same principles. His manz would have known to fill him in on them important details. Not letting him know was letting him go astray. In Cory's mind real dudes didn't let their manz fall for smuts, not without them knowing.

****

When Cory got off of work he seen that he had a few missed calls and text messages from Deron, Jenny and others. He waited until he got home then called Deron back.

"What's good bro."

"I was hitting you all night. Aint you on parole or something. It's nothing in them streets after twelve but trouble," Deron said being funny.

119

"But pussy, don't forget that because that's where I was at."

"Well look, I got something official for you. Ma lady want to know do you want to go out with her and her friend Asia? She feeling you bro."

"Come on man, I don't want none of ya girl uppity friends. You know how I'm on it. I love ma hood rats."

"They aint uppity. I'm talking about Asia, the one you was talking to that day we was over Philly."

"Her? She was nice. She seem cool, but I'm not really good with them kind of chicks. They be having unreal expectations. Some things I just aint willing to do or give up."

"Like what? It's not like she want to marry you. She don't even know you so what are you talking about?"

"I'm talking about all that extra stuff you be doing, pulling out chairs, opening doors. I aint doing none of that stuff if she could do it for herself."

"Man that's me, you aint got to do any of that. Just be who you are, either she like you or she don't. You thinking too hard. It's simple, ya'll go out if ya'll click then it lead to ya'll getting to know each other a little more, If not then that's it."

"You right, I be bugging. I don't like putting myself in uncomfortable situations."

"It's a lot of good things in life that you're going to miss out on if you don't be more open minded. You not in the drug game no more, you don't have to have ya guard up so much. You dealing with regular people now, live your life."

"You right. When we going out?"

"We're going to do a double date, everything on me."

"Good, because I'm kind of fucked up."

"How you fucked up? What do you be spending money on?"

"Clothes, everything high. A hundred plus for jean at least, then almost two for some Nikes, it's crazy. I was thinking about getting another job." Cory didn't want to tell him what he was really thinking about doing.

"Why don't you try getting a part time Job at one of the gyms. Be a personal trainer," Deron suggested. He knew the drastic measures dudes in the hood took when funds got low. Most of which led dudes right back behind the wall.

"That do make sense. I'll be able to work out when I want and make money. I might do that."

## Chapter 25

This was Cory's second double date which he thought was crazy. He never thought he'll ever be dating. That's something dudes didn't do where he was from. Well that he thought dudes didn't do. He didn't know that his friends who wasn't in the streets were moving different. He had gotten locked up young and wasn't accustomed to stuff like that. Being a real one he admitted to himself that he was kind of socially set back, he just didn't know how much.

Deron, Ebony, Asia, and Cory sat in Zeppoli, a little restaurant in Collingswood. It was an elegant spot. A family owned business. Cory didn't know how Deron found it but he commended him. The food was delicious. The place was packed and everyone was throwing down. Deron and Ebony was in there own little zone. Feeding one another, laughing, snuggling, being lovely dovey, displaying their love for the world to see. It kind of made things awkward for Cory and Asia. They sat across from them creating small talk.

Cory didn't really know how to come at Asia. Their first conversation at the concert was friendly, no expectations so it flowed with ease. Now he was hesitant, watching what he said. He could sense Asia was tired of the messing around. Once she realize that he was keeping it basic she turned the conversation on him.

"So what do you do Cory?"

Cory took a sip of his wine to help wash down the food he was chewing. Then gave his mouth a little dap with his napkin to seem elegant. He was green at dinning out but he saw enough movies to know how to conduct himself. Plus Deron being the good friend that he was checked him before they got there. Told him to act like a gentlemen, chew with his mouth shut. Cory wasn't offended when his manz pulled him up. He found it funny. Chewing with his mouth open was an unconscious ugly habit he had. Growing up he didn't have a mother or a father to correct that.

"I'm a HVAC technician," Cory responded to her question.

"What's that?"

"I'm the guy you call when your central air is not working right."

"Handy man, huh?"

"You could say that. I been thinking about becoming a personal trainer too. How about you, what are you into?"

"I'm a teacher and a community organizer."

"So you like to work with people," Cory asked wanting her to tell him more?

"I like to do things for my community. I feel like we need all the help we can get in Camden, don't you think?"

"Yeah," Cory agreed. That wasn't something he thought about before. He really didn't care. He was trying to survive and live life. That's what occupied his mind. He was feeling her vibe though. She seemed really positive and upbeat. He wondered if that was her regular or was she putting on for their date.

"Ebony and I are putting on a dance show this weekend for the young ladies in our foundation. Would you like to come? It's a chance for you to see a little of what I do."

"Yeah, I don't mind. What day is it?"

Cory was interested. He wanted to know more about her. She seemed genuine. Not like she was trying to present herself in the best light because they were on a date, or because she liked him. He felt like he was really getting to know her for her. He didn't have any expectations of getting in her pants. He only went on the date because Deron told him to be more open.


## Chapter 26

Since Asia and Ebony was putting on the show Cory knew that his manz Deron would be there. He haven't seen him since the double date. He figured he'll surprise him. The place was packed with kids, there were parents seated waiting on the performance to start. Cory dressed regular for the occasion. A pair of blue and white Air Max 90's blue jeans and a grey zip up hoodie. He didn't have much in his closet for going out. Deron had to help him pick something out the day of the double date. He called himself sneaking up on Deron while he was talking to Ebony.

"What's good money," Cory said with a big smile on his face.

"You think I'm surprised to see you here. I'm not, I knew you was coming. Why you late?"

"How you doing Ebony," Cory said ignoring Deron. He gave her a little handshake.

"I'm okay, and yourself?"

"I'm good."

"Cory, you made it."

Cory turned around to a warm hug that he wasn't quite ready for. Asia hugged him like she missed him. He felt her head lay against his chest. He hugged her back looking at Ebony and Deron. They were both smiling.

"I'm glad you made it," She said never letting go of his waist. You're just in time. Come on, let me show you to your seat," She grabbed his hand and led him towards the front. Cory looked back at Deron. Deron shrugged his shoulders tilting his head to the side a little. Asia was excited to have him there. She took him to their front row seats. "I'll be right back," she said hurrying off. Cory sat down looking around. Deron came and sat next to him.

"She big on you bro. You a lucky man."

"Whatever miss me with that mushy stuff," Cory responded to Deron.

The smile left Deron's face instantly. "Alright angry man," Deron said turning around in his chair.

The lights got dim, the show begun. Asia and Ebony came and sat near their men.

All of a sudden the stage lit up. These young boys came running on stage from the right, at the same time some young girls ran on stage from the left. They ran through one another in their African garments, flipping, and dancing. One kid chatting something in an African language. Africa was the theme, the backdrop was the jungle. Four kids were on stage beating African drums while the youths danced barefoot. All of them in sync. The drums had Cory's shoulders wanting to jump but he held them still. The drums stopped. All the kids ran off stage. Seconds later a few of them came out and started performing the play.

Cory was impressed at how good it was. It was one thing after another. The whole event exceeded his expectations. He enjoyed himself a lot more than he thought he would.

The last skit this cute little girl came on stage reading from a piece of paper. What she was reading was kind of profound. It was talking about life and it's lessons. Cory thought that was kind of ironic because she didn't know anything about either. She still has yet to get her first life lesson.

When she was finished the curtains closed bringing the spectacle to an end. All the kids came back on stage together bowing. The crowd gave a long drawn out standing ovation. The lights came on as parents made their way to the stage to hug and congratulate their kids. The feeling reminded Cory of when he was young in school watching plays in the auditorium. He didn't participated in any. That wasn't what the cool kids did. Now thinking back he realized he had a loser mentality even then.

"Come on, I want to introduce you to some people," Asia said dragging him off.

They went backstage with the people who did mostly everything, the dance instructors etc.… Asia and Ebony were the hands that put everything together, but they had a lot of people behind the scenes that was making it happen. Their crew was cleaning and packing up. Asia had got caught in a conversation. Cory seen Deron helping out so he went over there to mess with him.

"You mean to tell me this what you been up to on the low," Cory said so only Deron could hear him. Deron was laughing while putting trash in the trash bag he held. "It's amazing what some good twot can do."

"You funny as hell. Tell me you wasn't feeling that play," Deron said.

"I liked it. They did a good job, but you know what I'm talking about Mr. Sucka For Love." Cory joined in on the cleaning process while joking with Deron. After everything was cleaned up he went over to Asia. "How you getting home," he asked her?

"Ebony and I have a van full of stuff that we have to get back. Why are you smiling at me like that," Asia playfully asked?

"Nothing," Cory lied. His smile was close mouth. He was amused by how cute she was and how proper she spoke.

"Did you like it," she asked?

Cory nodded his head. "I really enjoyed myself."

"Well, I'm glad you did."

"I have to go get ready for work tomorrow. Since you don't need me to take you home I assume you'll be alright."

"I'll be fine."

"Alight, give me a call or something to let me know you made it home safe." Cory said and gave her a hug before leaving.


## Chapter 27

Kimberly was seated at her desk in her cubicle typing while taking a call on her head set when the job's mail carrier walked up with some flowers. All the women were looking trying to see where he was going to stop at with the flowers he was carrying. When they saw where he stopped at she became the envy of all of their jealousy.

Kimberly looked up then pointed to herself asking, "for me," in a silent voice? She didn't want the caller in her headset to think that she was talking to her. The carrier nodded his head and gave her a paper to sign. She signed it while still talking. The carrier set them on her desk and left. She was blushing on the inside and out. She already assumed who they were from. When she was done with her caller she grabbed the bouquet, admired them, smelled them, then found the card. While reading it a big smile appeared on her face. When she looked up Ja'neece was standing right there.

"Look at you, over here smiling like crazy. Who are they from?"

"They're from E.J.. Aint they sweet?"

"He seem sweet. A little old fashion but I'll take that all day over these lames out here," Ja'neece stated.

"No one has ever given me flowers before."

"I can tell. Let me get back to work. I'll talk to you in a bit," Ja'neece said before leaving.

After receiving them flowers Kimberly couldn't function right anymore. She kept thinking about E.J.. She had finally met a good guy. She knew her mother would approve of him. Then she thought it would be a good idea to introduce him to her mother.

## Chapter 28

Ed was the owner of the Gym Cory attended. A short cocky Italian guy who always had a story whenever he saw Cory or his friends. He was cool with E.J. that's how him and Cory became fly. Cory had asked him for a part time job and got hired on the spot. Cory would go to work at the HVAC company, go home take a shower change then head back out to the gym. The gym didn't feel like work because working out was something that he liked doing. He would work out and help other people workout. It seemed like once all the ladies found out that he was now a trainer all of a sudden they didn't know how to use the machines. He didn't mind, it was his job. He flirted, a couple of them wanted to go out but he didn't have time in his schedule unless they just wanted to smash. He always made time to get some pussy.

Lately Jenny and Eve had been the only females he been dealing with. He hadn't seen or talk to Asia since the night of the play. He reached out to her a couple of times but didn't get an answer. Since she wasn't fucking he seen it as her saving him the wasted time. He wasn't one to put in a lot of effort to get some sex. He had a variety of ladies at the gym jockeying for position. They wanted to fuck so that just push Asia further to the back of his mind.

Kimberly and her friend would come to the gym a few times a week. On the strength of E.J. they'll speak to Cory. He would give them friendly conversation and help if they needed any. At times Cory a see the muscle head dude talking to Kimberly. Her and her friend always looked uninterested. Cory didn't know if it was because he was there or not. It didn't matter he was obligated to let his manz know but after the second time it was no use unless she got caught doing something out of pocket.

Cory had gotten to know dude a little. One day while working out by himself dude came over there wanting to join the workout. While they were working out dude began offering these unwanted workout tips on how to work certain muscles. All this stuff Cory wasn't beat for. It reminded him of when he was in prison, it would always be that one dude, more than likely an old head who was always trying to show somebody how to work out or hit the bag but his weight piece wasn't right and his hands wasn't sharp.

****

"I haven't heard from him in almost two weeks now," Asia said.

"Did you try calling him," Ebony asked?

"I tried twice. I left a message once, still haven't heard anything back."

"I'll ask Deron about him."

"Maybe I'm not his type."

"Why you say that?"

"I don't know, why else wouldn't he call me? That's the only reason I can think of."

Ebony and Asia were walking through the mall with their bags in hand going from store to store.

"I could tell you really like him. I never seen you bothering yourself thinking about a man how you are now."

Asia began giggling letting Ebony know that she was right.

"It's something about him. I don't know what it is. I'm still trying to figure him out. He's reserved like he's protecting himself from something. We would be having a good conversation, good laughs but it'll be surface talk. I feel like it's a door that he's locking me out of."

"Maybe you should ask him more intimate questions, things you really want to know about him."

130

"I will if I get a chance to. I didn't want to get personal on them other dates. I more so wanted to have a good time, become friends first."

"I know what you're trying to do, but he seem like a different type of guy. He seem more you know, humm." Ebony was trying to find the word. "Street," She finally said. "You could do that with the guys at the office but a guy like him you have to at least dangle the goods in his face while making him work for it. All the while ya'll getting to know one another. Don't get me wrong I'm not saying give him some to keep him around. Show him the fun he'll miss out on if he don't stick around. Then let him fantasize about it. I bet he'll work for it. Trust me I know."

"I hope he not the type with only getting some on his mind," Asia said.

"That's all that occupies every man's mind."

"I know that's why I need a guy who likes me for me. Now if we get to that aye, I like getting my freak on too. I just don't want to be treated like a piece of meat. I won't disrespect myself for anyone. I like him. I see everything I want in my man in him. He got the hood in him but he not in the streets. He seem like a gentleman. I also see a little sadness when I look in his eyes. I would like to know what's that about."

"What Asia, you want a thug," Ebony joked?

"Not a thug. I don't want somebody that's robbing and killing people or that's getting locked up. I like the edge he got to him. I would say swag but everybody with tight jeans and funny haircuts say they got swag. I see him as a man."

"What you think you can save or change him, cause you know what they say?"

"No nothing like that. I want to show him what it's like to have a strong black woman by his side. If the black man only knew the heights he could achieve with a good woman. They don't know that their powers would be limitless."

Asia was what some may call pro black. She wouldn't call herself that, she just loved to help her people in any way she could. It was how she was raised. Her parents were real conscious people. They taught her the importance of family and community service. They were always involved in the community. She was raised helping others. It became a way of life for her. Her parents made giving back fun and interesting. They taught her how to love and appreciate life and what she was blessed with. They taught her black history, how to be self-sufficient, to never make excuses or play the victim and how to love the skin she was in.

Asia parents taught her many things that she would carry throughout life. Living in the hood always kept her asking questions when she was younger. Her parents would always let her know that the world wasn't perfect neither was the people in it but if she kept contributing in a positive way that it'll become a better place. Even as a little girl they would let her know how important she was to her community. That's why she always felt strongly about black on black crime and guys destroying their neighborhood with drugs. It's one of the reasons she became a teacher, so she could play her part in helping mend the broken school system. Camden had a 65% drop out rate. She figured that it would be wise to try to get to the youth before the streets did. That's what she tried to do through her teachings, community services and organizing.

## Chapter 29

Jenny stood by the bed buttoning up her shirt while talking to Cory who was still lying in bed. She leaned over and gave him a kiss on the lips then said, "I'll call you."

"Alright," Cory replied while looking through his phone. He didn't like kissing but that was Jenny's thing. While having sex he didn't quite mind. Any other time the freaky things she might be doing with her man popped into his mind. Just off the things him and her did in the little time they knew one another, he could only image the things she did with a dude who she been having sex with for years.

Cory had set his cell phone down and went to the bathroom. While coming out his phone had rang. Jenny quickly picked it up out of reaction. Before she put it to her ear two say anything she turned around and saw Cory staring at her like an evil man on a scary movie. That's when she realized she was out of pocket.

"Give me my phone, I don't answer your phone when I'm over your house, do I?"

Jenny gave him the phone with a smile on her face.

"Hello." He put his hands over the mouthpiece of the receiver just in time to block out Jenny saying goodbye. He said "bye," and she left. For some reason Cory had mixed feelings about hearing the voice on the other end of the phone. It was a pleasant voice that he was trying to avoid for reasons he didn't quite know.

"Hey Asia."

"You're hard to get in contact with," she said.

"I've been working a lot. I got another job at the gym. Working two jobs be like my whole day. After work I be drained."

"It's good to know that I'm not the reason you haven't called."

"It's not you, why would you say that?"

"I'm not used to a guy not being the pursuer."

"I figure you wouldn't miss me, you're beautiful, smart and probably have plenty of guys pursuing you."

"I appreciate the compliments, but that's not the case."

"You really mean to tell me that there's no man in your life?"

"Nope, if there was I wouldn't be talking to you right now. I'm not that kind of woman."

Cory couldn't believe her if he wanted to. In his mind there wasn't a woman walking around that wasn't getting dick or in some cases pussy.

"Instead of asking you to go out with me if I had a man I would have just gone out with him, right?"

"Oh, you're asking me out?"

"Sure, It's poetry night Wednesday over Philly. I wanted to know would you like to come with me?"

Cory thought about it for a second. He wasn't into poetry but was open to going there with her."

"What time do it start," Cory asked knowing he had to work on Wednesday?

"It starts at 6:00 o'clock PM. They're going to start performing around eight."

"I'll go with you, I'm off of work before 6."

They had set the date up. Cory laid back smiling as he thought about how relentless Asia was. *Poetry*, he thought. He never met a female like Asia. She was into different things than females he was used to. He respected her on another level. In the back of his mind he knew she wasn't the one for him.

****

Wednesday night Asia came to pick Cory up. Cory didn't really know what to wear for an occasion like this so he put on some jeans, a sweater, and some tan construction timberlands. When they arrived at the spot Asia got out of the car and seen Cory smiling to himself.

"What," Asia asked?

"I was just thinking about how nice you look." While away Cory had come up with his own set of principles and one of them was not to give out too many compliments or let women know what he was really thinking or feeling. That way they'll stay on edge guessing, trying to figure him out, impress him or get his approval. He had to keep it real with Asia though, she looked stunning.

She had on a pink and white skirt that fitted her properly. He liked how she carried herself. Her manners, her style, it was no comparison to what he knew. She didn't know it but she was changing his perspective on a lot of things, challenging his beliefs.

Cory was expecting to see Maxwell and Erica Badoo type people there. While there was a few, there was also people of all colors, sizes, and styles.

"Not what you expected, huh," Asia asked seeing how he was observing others?

"I didn't know so many different kind of people liked poetry."

"Poetry is universal. It allows people express themselves in ways they might not be otherwise able to. Like a singer or rapper."

Cory had looked over at the stage. A man had went out there and was adjusting the microphone. The words Warm Daddy's was displayed over top of him. The dim light had set the scene for all the couples having a romantic diner. All the lights were on the stage. That's where Cory gave his undivided attention. It seem like that's where everyone attention was because the chattering came to a halt. Dude background music came on and he began his poem. Dude was an animated poet. Walking back and forth, feeding the crowd his energy. Afterwards everyone applauded.

"That was nice, I like that," Cory said applauding.

"You think you could do it?"

"I aint saying that now. I never tried. Plus public speaking isn't really my thing."

"You should try it one day."

"Maybe, one day," Cory said smirking knowing he had no intentions on ever going on that stage.

A few minutes after that guy left the stage a lady did her poem. Then came a guy with a guitar who sat on a stool. The night was entertaining. The poems were good. Some deeper than others. Cory started to feel like if he really tried he could make a good poem. Deep down he felt like he could do anything that he put his mind to. He was right but he didn't know it, he was still boxed in holding onto the street mentality.

"Where are you going," Cory asked Asia as she got up?

"I'll be back," Asia said with an assuring smile.

He figured she was going to the restroom but she led his eyes onto the stage.

"This poem is called (A love you should know).

A prize, a jewel in the crown of any king,

Conflicted in my pursuit of happiness but I know he's the one for me,

His presence is a present, his time he gifts to me,

Intriguing personality and funny as can be,

Enigmatic and energetic, conversations without effort,

Respecting his thoughts and opinions and loving that he's different,

His powers are conserved and hidden under hurt,

His past dies out so his destiny could give birth,

A real one recognizes a king even when he's in the field,

Seeing pass the dirt and the grit she knows a kingdom is being built….

Cory listened to every word assuming that they applied to him. The poem could have been taking general. Other guys in there could have been feeling the same way because of how it was written. A good poet lays it out there in a way that makes other people feel their words. While Asia was reciting the poem one woman shouted out amen, another said preach girl. Other women nodded their heads in agreement.

Cory sat at their little table by himself listening to her every word. He didn't even bother to look at the waitress who came and collected their plates. He was too busy thinking about Asia's words. The crowd applauded Asia as she came off the stage. Cory stood up clapping harder.  Contradicting himself in so many ways he pulled her chair out for her as she came back to the table.

"Thank you," she said.

Cory took her hand and didn't let it go as they sat down. He held it over the little table as they sat across from one another. Asia was blushing, she could tell that he liked her poem before he even said it.

"I really liked that poem."

"Thanks."

"It was deep. I felt like everything applied to me."

"Well, you know that's what good poems does. They resonate with the audience you trying to capture."

"What inspired it?"

"Someone who I consider a friend."

138

"Oh," Cory said sounding disappointed. He let go of her hand and leaned back in the chair.

"I was talking about you silly," she said grabbing his hand back.

"I know, I just wanted you to say it," Cory said playing his little joke on her.

Cory was glad to have inspired the poem. He didn't know that he was having that kind of effect on her. The rest of the night he was mushy, opening up to her as they gotten to know one another. When the night was over they ended up parked in front of his house talking.

Cory seat was leaned back. He had his arm around her chair which was sitting up right close to the steering wheel how most women drive. They were looking at one another talking.

"Would you like to come in."

"No, I have to work tomorrow, but I'll take a rain check."

"So when is the next time I'm going to see you?"

"Whenever you find time. You the one who don't be getting back to me," Asia said.

"You right you right. That won't happen again."

"If you say so," she replied.

They hugged and Cory went in the house. While out on his date he had his phone on airplane mode so he didn't get any of his calls even though as he looked at his phone now he could see who had called him. He read a text from Deron that said, "Yo bro, get at me ASAP." He called him immediately.

"Hello."

"What's good, I got ya text."

Cory's phone call couldn't have come at a worse time. Deron was in the middle of making love to his girl. When he answered the phone he rolled over on his back. Ebony didn't stop, she took the top position, kissing him all on the face and neck.

"You blowing ma shit right now. We'll talk tomorrow."

"You getting ya rocks off."

"Chill bro."

"Alright, I'm out." Click!

Cory spent the rest of the night thinking about Asia. He woke up and went to work with her still on his mind. He wasn't too fond that thoughts of her was taking his mind prisoner but he couldn't help it. She had left a good impression on him. Now his subconscious was trying to figure her out. Thoughts of being in a relationship with her were automatically coming to him. Even when he tried to mentally trash them they'll pop back up. She was unlike any female he had ever been with. He wondered if a relationship with her a be demanding, if so how demanding. Would he be giving up his freedom? Will he be missing out or gaining?

It seemed like everything Asia had said in that poem was true. Not only about him but a lot of other dudes as well. His whole life he had been running from commitment. Mainly because he didn't believe in peoples conventional way of living. He was determined to live life on his own terms, not how society expected.

\*\*\*\*

"One more minute. Go faster so you can feel the burn," Cory told the lady he was training. He was standing on the side of the bike while she was riding. While waiting for her to finish her last minute he saw E.J. and Deron come in the gym.

"That's a good workout," he said handing her a towel so she could dry her sweat off with. "I'll see you Monday."

"Yeah Monday," she responded with the little breath she could muster up.

He lightly patted her sweaty back and left her there looking exhausted.

"Ok bro, that's you right there," E.J. joked?

"Stop trying to play me. I'm getting her ready for her big day." You should be worried about ma man that keep pushing up on ya chick," Cory said.

"I'ma talk to him today. Enough is enough, I'm starting to feel disrespected." Even though E.J. was big and burly his words didn't carry any threats.

"What's good with you bro, you kind of quiet," Cory said sitting on the bench. He began moving his arms back and forth warming up to do his set of presses while looking at Deron curiously.

"Asia been asking about you. Let me find out that you running from her."

"Come on now, me running from her." Cory laughed what Deron had said off as if it didn't deserve a response. "I don't know what you talking about."

"You know what I'm talking about. You always running from the right ones, not the wrong ones. Anyone that might challenge you or who you think aint going to put up with ya shit."

Deron looked upset. Cory began smirking because he was getting to see what Deron really thought. He couldn't get mad because he knew his manz only wanted what he thought was best for him. He knew that he didn't know what he was talking about. Cory let him finish talking and calmly said, "we went out last night. That's where I was coming from when I called you." Cory laid down on the bench and began pushing the weight.

"You sat there with that stupid smirk on ya face and let me say all that. Where ya'll go?"

"Warm Daddy's over Philly," he said once he racked the barbell and got up from the bench. "It was nice. They had poetry night there."

Deron eyes lit up with surprise when Cory said that it was nice. He didn't think he was into stuff like that. "I been there before with Ebony. You liked it, huh?"

"Yeah, it was different. She did a poem for me. I wasn't even expecting it."

"She feeling you, don't mess it up."

"I know, it's kind of scary."

"You like her?"

"Yeah, but…."

"Everything after but is bullshit. I already know how you coming. Just let things play itself out and see where they go," Deron suggested.

"You right," Cory said nodding his head in agreement.

Deron knew him better than anybody. Even while giving his sincere advice he was thinking watch he mess it up. "Where this guy at," Deron asked looking around.

It was on E.J. to do a set but while they were talking he slid off to the other side of the gym to approach the muscle bound dude who kept trying to push up on Kim.

"I just wanted to let you know that's my woman. I'll appreciate if you stop trying to talk to her," E.J. told dude.

Dude knew what it was when E.J. wanted to talk to him. He didn't approach him aggressively but dude still had that nervous look in his eyes. After E.J. finish saying what he had to say dude said, "I don't want any problems. You got it." Dude put out his hand for a handshake. E.J. shook his hand then stepped off. When he turned around to walk off he saw both of his manz over there looking at him. He kept a serious face on as he walked back over to their workout area.

"Yo, when he stuck out his hand I tapped Deron like I know he aint about to fall for the old handshake and hook move. I thought we was going to have to run over there," Cory joked with E.J. when he came back.

"Nah, he said he didn't want any problem. Gotta respect it."

"Spence want us to get fitted for them tuxedos next week. He said that he can't wait until this wedding is over. She driving him crazy," Deron told the fellas.

"I bet she is. Chicks be thinking that it's only their day. They don't give the man a say in anything. The dude is getting married too, feel me," Cory said.

Either responded. They looked at each other with a smirk knowing not to get him started. "It's on you," Deron told E.J.. E.J. laid on the bench and Deron stood at the head of the bench as his spot.

"Oh ya'll going to leave me hanging, huh?" Cory had his arms out because he knew that they were on some other stuff. He found it funny though. His boys knew how he be acting like a Heman woman hater so to avoid any heated discussions they didn't even feed into them.

## Chapter 30

Cory called Asia a little after 8:00 O'clock at night. At the second ring she picked up sounding like a goddess. Everything about Asia was sweet and feminine. She had a genuinely pleasant disposition. What Cory liked most was the mental stimulation he received when vibing with her. It was always something to look forward to, something new to find out. Not only about her but anything she would put him on.

"What's up little lady?"

"Hey Cory."

"How did you know it was me?"

"I know your voice by now. Plus not too many people call my phone this time of night, especially guys."

"That's good to know. What you doing?"

"Sitting on the couch watching T.V. petting my cat."

"Don't tell me you one of them crazy ladies with like ten cats running around ya house."

"No, I only have one. Why, you don't like cats?"

"I don't have a problem with them. Pets just demand too much attention. If I get anything it's going to be like a goldfish or something. That way I don't have to do much."

Cory could hear her giggling over the phone.

"You're funny. Cats are pretty independent," Asia said through her giggles.

"I wish I could see that smile right now. Do you live by yourself.?"

"Yup."

"I know you get lonely sometimes."

"That's why I got kitty right here."

"That's ya cat name?"

"Uh hum."

"So what happened to the guy that used to keep you company on them lonely nights?"

"I haven't had one of them in a while. It seem like I always end up dating selfish idiots who think the world revolves around them."

Cory's eyebrows went up. That sounded like him to the tee. He took a mental note not to let his past experiences with women dictate how he was going to deal with Asia. So far she was showing to be different so he knew he had to come different. The fact that he didn't want to be placed in that category of dudes she had just described let him know that he was really into Asia.

"What about you?"

"I haven't had a real relationship in over twelve years," Cory answered.

"Why so long?"

"It's a long story," he said not wanting to explain.

"Well I still have a couple hours before I go to bed, unless you just don't want to talk about it."

Cory didn't feel like he had anything to hide. Any female he dealt with he knew eventually the subject would come up.

"I don't mind. I did a ten year bid. That's basically when the relationship ended."

"You did ten years in prison? Wow, that's a lot of time. How long have you been home?"

Shocked or fascinated she was coming back to back with questions without letting him get a word in between.

"A couple of years," he responded after she let him talk. I aint going back either."

"That's good to know. It's a shame that so many black men are locked up. Some of ya'll don't understand how much ya'll are needed out here."

Asia started going in about the state of the black man, about the racists system, the subliminal racist monuments throughout the country and how to gradually change things for the better. She spoke with passion and gave it to him like an educator. She put a time lime on the events she spoke about. That's how he knew she knew her stuff. The whole time while listening all he could think about was how different she was.

The next few days they spoke on the phone almost every night. Little by little Cory began opening up to her. He told her the story about how his ex dissed him when he was locked up. How his mom passed away when he was young, and that the only family he had was Deron, E.J., and Spence. Cory wasn't looking for sympathy. It just so happen that his story was a sad one. On the other hand, Asia's story was cotton candy sweat. Still they swapped stories laughing and joking while staying up all night on the phone like they were back in the sixth grade.

They both were busy people yet they found time to go out on a few dates. Cory felt like Asia understood him. While with her he didn't only think about getting some pussy how he did with other women. Her conversation was actually intriguing. He would lavish her with compliments on her appearance every time he saw her but it was her mind that would take him to places he have yet to go.

He found himself being a complete gentlemen in her presence. Opening doors for her and not feeling out of character doing so. Things he never thought he'll be doing but a change was taking place within. One he wasn't quite aware of.

One time Asia invited him to go with her to the zoo. At first he was hesitant thinking about how elementary the zoo sounded but he went anyway. It was there he realized that time with her was always beautifully spent. That it wasn't about the place they went but about their time together. While there she clung to him, holding his hand. Public affection wasn't displayed like this where Cory was from, from men or women. In many ways where they were from the women were like the dudes, but Asia was different. She was raised different, she had a heart of gold. One that Cory couldn't see himself taking advantage of even if he wanted to.

The feelings was mutual and it reflected in their bond. Asia seen the good in Cory. She seen things in him that he didn't see in himself. She seen a strong man who had been through some things. Every chance she got she would let him know that his past didn't define him, and that his future was bright. She knew that if his strength was focused on the right things that it would become an unstoppable force.

Side by side they walked snacking on their slushies and pretzels while observing the wildlife in captivity. Seeing the big bad Gorilla in that cage looking pitiful reminded Cory of his time behind bars. He didn't like it. That same sight caused Asia to ask Cory a theoretical question. "Do you believe we evolved from apes?"

"Nah, I can't go with that. If we evolved from them how come they're not still evolving. I think we evolved mentally and socially. The only physical evolving we probably did was start walking up right. I believe we continue to evolve with every piece of knowledge we get and apply. Some people evolve faster than others."

Asia was smiling on the inside. She didn't have a comeback. She didn't believe we came from monkeys either. That wasn't why he had her smiling though. He had impressed her with his answer. Not only did he cause her to see the human evolution theory from a different perspective but it was something in what he said that caused her to see the hood differently. She was entrenched in helping the community and he helped her see another method to contribute to that process.

They continued on their stroll ending up where the lions were. They seen the biggest lion over there looking defeated laying there in the corner with a face uncharacteristic of that of the king of the jungle.

"What do you think of animals being took out of their natural habitat," Asia asked Cory?

"I never really thought about it, why?"

"It's just a question."

"You know in America it always come down to money. Everything is entertainment here. That's all this is."

Asia nodded her head in agreement. "Sometimes I wish I could know what these animals are thinking because I know they do some kind of thinking. Do you ever wonder?"

"It probably crossed my mind before. You be asking some weird questions," Cory joked.

"Nah-un," she said. They both started laughing. Cory put his right arm around her hugging up with her. They both stared at the lion who could never share their humor.

## Chapter 31

That Monday Spence came from Atlantic City to Camden and him and the fellas went and got their suits fitted. As soon as Cory seen the color of the suits he had something to say.

"Why you got us wearing all these fruity colors? I feel like a laughy taffy wearing this color blue," Cory joked.

"Ma fiancé picked the colors out. She wanted everything color coordinated. I'm just going along with it. You know happy wife happy life."

"Bullshit," Cory shot back. "That's just some shit that rhyme."

Deron and E.J. was laughing. They was expecting that kind of response and Cory didn't disappoint.

"Hold champ, be careful down there," Cory told the tailor who was taking the measurements of his inseams.

"What's up with you and Asia," Deron asked? "I heard ya'll been going out a lot."

"We went out a couple of times," Cory said nonchalantly trying to brush the question off.

"You like her? Keep it real too, don't be trying to act hardbody."

"I'm digging her," Cory admitted.

"I heard ya'll went to the zoo," Deron said with a smirk on his face.

"Dam, do Ebony tell you everything?"

"That's what's up though. I was afraid you was going to try to say that she aint ya type. You know anything that don't fuck on the first date aint your type."

"She different though," Cory said in a low exciting tune. It kind of shocked everybody. That's why I'm feeling her. We do things and talk about stuff I never thought I'll be doing or talking about. She real vibrant. She put her heart and soul into the things she do. I think that's what got me. It's attractive."

"I have to meet this women. I never heard you speak of a woman like this before. Let me find out my boy getting soft," E.J. joked.

"He not getting soft, he falling in love," Spence followed up.

"I wouldn't say all that bro, but I do think I'ma need an extra invitation so I can bring her to ya wedding."

"You got it," Spence replied.

E.J. chimed in. "I'm going to need one too." He wanted to bring Kim.

"I'm not going to lie, for the first time in a long time I been thinking about settling down," Cory said smiling looking at his boys for their reactions. He was done getting fitted. E.J. was next.

"Having a companion is a beautiful thing. Aint nothing like love, being loved, having that special lady you can trust. Especially if you know she one hundred with you," Spence said indirectly describing his situation.

"See that's ma thing, you never know if they're one hundred with you until shit hit the fan, but by then it's too late. That's why I'ma have to put her through ma three phase test."

"You got a test you be putting chicks through bro," E.J. asked laughing?

Deron smacked his forehead like the emoji, turned around and began shaking his head. "Why this guy just can't be human like everybody else," Deron asked god?

"Hell yeah," Cory said responding to E.J.. "It's something I came up with while I was down. I stay hitting these chicks with it. Aint none past yet. One time I let this chick steal $50 from me. Petty shit, all she had to do was ask I would of gave it to her. Nah, I'm lying. I wouldn't have gave her shit. That's beside the point though, I blame myself because I know the kind of chicks I be dealing with so the test be like a waste of time."

"You can't play with love bro, you can end up missing out. Sometimes you just have to take a leap of faith," Spence said warning Cory. If Cory really was dealing with a good woman Spence didn't want to see him lose her by acting childish.

"I aint playing, I'm dead serious. I aint got no time to be taking a leap of faith, I need to know for sure. I know chicks a play their parts until they get what they want or their way then they'll flip the script. I know these things bro. I could only hope she not like that.

## Chapter 32

Ebony and Asia was at the community center where after work they spent most of their time empowering young women. It was the home of their Lovely ladies foundation. There were other staff members who volunteered but as the head of the organization they split the only office between the two of them.

Their office was never closed to anyone. Usually a staff member a be in there talking about an issue or a topic. At the present moment Asia and Ebony was straightening up before leaving.

"Did Cory tell you about a wedding their friend is having?"

"No, he hasn't said anything about a wedding," Asia responded.

"Deron invited me yesterday. Here go the invitation right here." Ebony reached out handing Asia the invitation. "It's cute, aint it?"

"Yes it is. This the other guy Deron was with at the music festival. "They're a cute couple," Asia complimented looking over the invitation. A hint of jealousy sat in her stomach but she wasn't sure if she should even be feeling it. "I don't know if we're at that point when he would invite me to a wedding."

"Why you say that?"

"I don't know, it might be too soon. We just really getting to know one another. You know guys, the only part they like to rush is when their trying to get some."

"You not lying about that," Ebony responded.

"I invited Cory to the DeAngelo Bey conference coming up. He going to be talking about love. That brother deep, I want him to hear some of what he has to say. Are you coming?"

"Girlllll, you think you slick. I see what you up to."

"What you talking about," Asia asked with a little innocent slick smirk on her face.

"It seem like you trying to groom Cory into the man you want him to be. You have to be careful, that maybe what be scaring the guys in your relationships off. Everybody is not into what we're into."

"You right but I don't think that's what I'm doing. I hope he don't see it that way. I see it as me inviting him into my world. These are places and things I'm going to do without a date. I'm showing him the kind of woman I am. If that scares him off then he's not the one for me."

Ebony agreed.

"I could tell that he would probably have never went to any of these spots if I never took him but to my surprise it seem like he likes them. I also see it as an opportunity for us to spend more time together and get to know one another. Experience things together so we can have more to talk about. He got different views. He see the world differently but you'll never know because he keeps his opinions to himself. That's why I'm always asking him questions. I like to hear his perspective on things."

"What do you mean he see the world differently?"

"He sees things through his own experiencing. Deron didn't tell you that he did ten in prison before?"

"No, He didn't. You know I would have told you that before trying to set ya'll up," Ebony assured her.

"It's alright, it's not an issue. He a good guy. We talked about all of that."

"Ten years, that's a lot of time to be in prison. I can't imagine. How long has he been home?"

"About two years now."

"Does he seem awkward, like institutionalized? I'm asking because a lot of them guys be messed up after all that time and they don't even be knowing it."

"He's regular, but after so many years of living in a cage a lion no longer believes he is a lion. Likewise, after so many years in prison a man forgets how to be a man. Sometimes it takes a woman to let him know that he's still the king of the jungle."

Asia drew the analogy from thinking back on that sad lion they saw when they were at the zoo.

****

Cory tossed and turned before opening his eyes. He had a reoccurring nightmare. One where he was on a hill, he seen a preacher about to wed a couple next to a grave. For some reason he always ran down the hill towards the bride. Every time he got close to her she'll rip her veil off revealing the most hideous face. He'll always wake up at that point.

This was a nightmare he'll have every once in a while. At first it used to give him chills. He used to be trying to figure out the meaning but now he didn't think much of it.

After laying there for a while he fell back into a slumber. This time having dreams about making love to Asia. He dreamt of them kissing on a couch, then the scene skipped to him making love to her on a bed. His dream felt so good and so real that it caused him to have a wet dream.

"Oh shit," he said waking up out of his sleep. He sat up and pulled the covers back. When he looked down he had juzz on his thigh. He got up and went to the bathroom. In the shower he was thinking how the last time he had a wet dream was when he was locked up and that was because he wasn't getting any. In the same thoughts he thought about how he haven't been getting any.

Cory got out of the shower with the intentions of calling one of his chicks up. He had been messing with Asia for months now, the only stimulation he got from her was mentally. To have sex with a woman was nothing but for her to mentally stimulate him and keep him intrigued said a lot. The slow progress in their relationship was expected only because out of respect he didn't go at her how he did other females. Still he wasn't willing to wait for her to give in for him to get some.

While putting his under clothes on Cory looked over at the book Asia had given him. It laid there on the nightstand in the same position he'd left it the day she 'd given it to him. It was a Malcolm X book written by Alex Haley. Cory had always wanted to read it while in prison but never got the chance for whatever reason. He heard many guys talk about how good and inspiring it was. She had given it to him about a week ago. He didn't know if it's because she found out that Malcolm X did prison time and so did he, or what but he still have yet to crack it. Not doing so kind of made him feel bad. With the way she asked questions he knew that she'll have some questions soon. Not wanting to disappoint he picked the book up and laid there reading until he fell back asleep.

**\*\*\*\***

The day of the seminar the event was packed. Cory didn't expect a turn out like this for a seminar. Maybe the Essence music Festival, but to hear someone speak. *He must be a big deal,* Cory thought then wondered *how come he never heard of him.* It seemed like Asia was mingling in a different society then what he was used to. As he looked around he noticed the women out numbered men about eight to one. Even with Asia on his arm he kept catching them looking his way. *If only dudes could see all these beautiful women,* Cory thought to himself. All of them were looking good, smelling good, and dressed to impress. These weren't the type of women he was used to. These were the type his friends Deron, E.J., and Spence was used to. The self-help, goal motivated, family oriented, classy women who drank only wine, champagne, or martinis. Those were the drinks Asia was only interested in when they went out, and this was her environment so he kind of stereotyped everyone off of her. Cory didn't know but them seeing his type there was rare, that's why he was getting all them looks. They were used to suburban and professional guys. Even though he was dressed for the occasion, it was his swag and disposition that gave him up.

The two of them found their seats. Cory couldn't wait to see who this guy was telling all these beautiful women about love. As far as Cory was concerned this dude was trying to sell men out for a couple of dollars. Some images of a scruffy looking character with a big beard and a head full of hair popped up in Cory's mind. Only because them always seem to be the kind of guys that know how to love a woman properly, and they do it so well that the women seem to overlook the fact that them dudes don't do a good job of taking care of themselves.

157

Them thoughts were debunked as a tall light skin guy with wavy hair came out preaching about love. Trying to be mature Cory sat there listening, not wanting to be judgmental. He held back laughter on the outside but on the inside he was tickled. Cory looked around the room at the women hanging on to his every word. This guy had a cult like following.

Cory felt like dude was the reason females were looking for a man and couldn't keep one. He kept telling them that the man should always be trying to impress them when they went out. Cory was of the opinion that it wasn't about impressing anybody but the two should be in a constant state of learning one another. He believed that a man should be a gentleman but not other than himself.

Everything dude on stage was saying was about the man catering to the woman. Cory looked at the others then at Asia and realized that this guy was telling them exactly what he thought they wanted to hear. Cory slightly dropped his eyes and head in disappointment thinking, *this guy is setting them up for failure. Look at them though, this is what they want, they don't want the truth.* The speaker even recited a few verses from the scriptures and got some amens. He spoke for about an hour motivating, inspiring, and misleading them. At the end of it all he received a standing ovation. Some women wanted to take pictures with him, others wanted his autograph. Cory laughed to himself and shook his head in amazement. All he seen was a pimp who reversed the game.

"How did you like the seminar," Asia asked Cory on the drive home. She loved it and assumed he would too. Who wouldn't, it was about love.

"Truthfully, it sucked," Cory said with a smile. He took his eyes off the road for a split second to see her reaction. She stared back at him eyebrows raised.

"You serious?"

"You asked my opinion."

Asia appreciated his frankness. It was one of the things she liked most about him. He didn't put up a front or lie to make himself seem other than who he really was. She wasn't expecting that answer though. "Why do you feel like it sucked," Asia asked?

"It was a bunch of fluff. None of what he said had substance. He sent a bunch of women out to the world delusional. They're never going to find a man if they try to apply any of that stuff he was talking about."

Asia was a little disappointed that he didn't like it like she thought he would. Cory could sense it. He felt like he had to say something to make her ease up a little.

"I'm not saying that it was bad because it wasn't. It might be a lot of guys that agree with dude. I happen to see things differently. Being a strong independent woman is good, but you also have to let a man be a man. Don't try to change or shape him into your ideal man or fantasy. Especially when you're being fed mess like that. It's this simple, encourage a man to be himself with you and around you and if that's the man you fall in love with then that's the one for you. The check list and all that, women need to throw that out. I can't believe a man was telling ya'll to do all this. I thought this stuff was something women sit around and come up with. Reality is aint nobody perfect, every man is different, everybody love different. Some people love hard, some don't know how to express their love. I just kind of believe in accepting people for who they are not who you want them to be. To me that's true love."

Asia listened with the same intensity she had when she was at the seminar. Cory's perspective was just different but she valued it the same if not more. After he finished saying what he said she sat back and cracked a smile and repeated what he had said, "that's true love."

"Why you smiling like that," Cory asked?

"Cause, what do you know about true love?"

Without answering, Cory smirked and kept his eyes on the road.

"What kind of Woman do you want Cory," Asia asked?

A few months ago before he had really gotten to know her he would have been able to spit out an answer for her that was reflective of how cold his heart was. Things had changed now. She didn't know it but she changed his views on many things, especially women. He realized that his old views and narrow mindedness was shaped by his pass experiences. Taking him to different places and conversing about topics he never gave too much thought to helped open his mind.

The question sat on his mind. One thing he knew was that none of the females he dealt with in the past was his ideal woman. His mind went to her and all the respect and admiration he had for her and the things she do. She was any man's ideal woman, but it would have been too cliché for him to tell her that she was his ideal woman. Asia patiently waited looking at him as if to see the words literally come out of his mouth. "I want a real woman," he finally said.

"What do you mean by a real woman?"

"Someone loyal, genuine, sincere, who respect herself and holds herself up like yaself."

Asia was looking for a more detailed answer but he left her blushing and speechless. He wasn't trying to flatter her, he was serious. While trying to think of someone who fitted the bill she was the only person who kept popping up. She was his ideal woman. From how she looked, to how she dressed, to how she lived her life.

"I'll call you," Asia said when Cory parked in front of her house.

"Hold up," Cory said stopping her from exiting the car. "Can I get a kiss?" Cory felt like he played the nice guy role long enough, it was time to start pushing the envelope a little.

Asia smiled a closed mouth smile then leaned in and gave him a peck on the lips. She tried to pull back but Cory pulled her closer, and they began French kissing. It was a slow sensual kiss that sent tingles up Asia's spin causing the faucet between her legs to turn on. They were so into the kiss that Cory began thinking maybe that day he'll finally score. Then she pulled back. Their eyes burned with a desperate desire of one another.

"You want me to come up there to keep you company?"

"Maybe next time," Asia responded. She leaned in and gave him another peck on the lips then opened the door and hurried out of there before she had changed her mind.

"Hold up baby. Dag, you trying to run away from me. I been meaning to ask you would you like to go to this wedding with me? My friend getting married."

"I'll love to Cory. Let me know when, O.K.." She blew him a kiss and flashed a smile.

Cory leaned on the middle council watching her walk off. "Man, this chick playing," he told himself after looking down at his bulge.

After Asia entered the house she leaned back against the door looked up and exhaled.

## Chapter 33

"Look at her flirting with him. She been working out at this gym before me. Now that he became a trainer all of a sudden she need a personal trainer."

"You'll probably be doing the same thing if you was still looking for a man," Ja'neece told Kimberly.

"You right, who am I kidding," Kimberly said laughing at herself.

It seem like Kimberly and Ja'neece was doing more watching Cory train this Dominican lady than the leg workouts they were supposed to be doing.

"If you weren't married would you deal with him," Kimberly asked?

"I doubt it. I been stop messing with guys like him."

"What do you mean?"

"I mean Street guys. They don't commit and their not faithful. Girl, I learnt so many lessons dealing with them. Now I rather a square. I know his routine and I'll beat his ass if he get out of line."

Kimberly began cracking up laughing because Ja'neece was serious. She knew Ja'neece's husband, he did look like a weak back so she only could image her beating him up.

"E.J. did tell me he did ten years in prison. Supposedly he not in the streets anymore though."

"I can respect that, but crime and relationships are two different things. It take a different type of man to be faithful. I don't got him being the type."

"What do you think about E.J.," Kimberly asked?

"He seem like a good guy. You know him better than me. Good men are hard to find."

"You're right about that. He a good guy. He invited me to his friend wedding next month. You know the tall brown skin guy that comes in here with them every once in a while? He getting married. He some kind of corporate executive."

"See all the good ones are being put on lock. That's why I had to lock mines down. You better do the same and catch that bouquet," Ja'neece joked.


## Chapter 34

"I'm finish the book you gave me," Cory told Asia. He laid on the couch watching TV. Are you going to come get it?"

"You just trying to get me over there so you can try to get some."

"What's wrong with that? I know you want me as much as I want you."

Still playing hard to get Asia laughed his last comment off. Cory tried to play the humble guy who could look past the sexual aspect but that only worked for so long. Now he was trying her every chance he got. The thing was that she seem to be enjoying the whole cat and mouse thing.

"Did you like the book," Asia asked?

"Yeah," he answered.

"What did you like about it?"

On the other end of the phone Cory looked up to the sky and shook his head. He wasn't trying to give a verbal essay, but he didn't want to mess up the vibe they had going on so he played along.

"It was good, I learned some things about brother Malcolm."

"What was your favorite part," Asia drilled? She wanted to see if he really read it.

Cory began smiling because he did have a favorite part but it was one she would least aspect.

"My favorite part is when that hooker told him not to trust women."

"You mean to tell me that's your favorite part from that whole book."

"The whole thing was good, but that was my favorite part. Was you looking for anything specific?"

"I wasn't looking for anything specific, I was expecting something other than that though. Something positive, or up lifting. I gave it to you for inspiration. After you told me you did all that time I wanted you to see Malcolm struggles and how he became great. I wanted you to see that it's never too late, that your past don't have to define you or dictate your future. I wanted you to see that you could still do great things."

"Great things like what," Cory asked?

"Anything you put your mind to Cory. Like have you ever thought about telling your story to kids? You don't have to tell them your whole life, just the basic spiel that led you to the wrong path. Some of the bad choices you made that led you to prison. You can save countless lives."

"I never really thought about public speaking. I'm kind of shy when it comes to stuff like that."

"We can work on that, I'll help you."

"I'm not Malcolm X Asia, I don't have the passion to do that kind of stuff. I got one goal, that's to stay out of prison. Anything else is too much pressure. I don't like to make commitments."

"I know you not him, this is different. I work with a lot of youth, mostly girls but our young boys are running around tearing these streets up. They're the ones who truly need saving. They don't have any guidance, no father figures, not even someone to look up to who they respect. They're looking up to guys who are doing all the wrong things and who are taking advantage of them. They're going to lead them to an early grave."

"We need strong brothers to help make a change. Guys that's willing to mentor these boys, that's willing to help run some of these programs, be basketball, football, and boxing coaches. That's the kind of men these kids respect. We need men who won't give up on these boys. Their dying for father figures. Someone to show them how to be men and teach them about life. It's only so much us women can do. Half of their fathers are either dead or in prison. That's why we need someone like you, a strong black man who been through it. Who figured out that's not the life to live and decided to make a change for the better. Until we get this our boys are going to keep killing each other," Asia finished with her voice cracking.

"I could tell this is really dear to your heart." Cory could hear and feel the passion from her voice but what he couldn't see was the tears she was wiping from her eyes.

"You don't know the half Cory. I love doing things with these kids. The worst part is seeing the look in their eyes when they have to go home. They dread it. All I could do is pray for them because some of them are going home to physical and verbal abuse, neglect, to crack houses, no fathers, no food, a mother that parties every night, smoking and drinking and they are not their first priority. They're not being taught anything. It's really sad."

"I know how it is Asia. Them problems are going to always be there no matter what."

"What if Malcolm X thought like that, what if Martin Luther King thought like that, what if our ancestors thought like that? They fought to get us to the point we're at today. If they would have had that mindset we would have never made progress. You'll be surprised how you caring can effect a child.

That child could possibly become the next president, they'll always remember you. The person who cared when no one else did. The person who wouldn't give up on them when everyone else did. You'll be surprised."

Her preaching was touching Cory. He started thinking about the whole thing, maybe it wouldn't hurt for him to share his experience. Still he wasn't willing to make any promises. They kept talking and he told her that he would consider giving his spiel.

****

Cory seen this thing with Asia as another obstacle. He was trying to fuck and she wanted him to talk to some kids. It made him kind of regret telling her that he did all that time. It wasn't something he was proud of anyway which made it harder for him to tell his story. Over the days Asia stayed on him about it. He eventually agreed. She told him she wanted to fit him in at this event her and Ebony was putting together at the community center. She began helping him develop his spiel, giving him suggestions, and going over the presentation and everything with him. Cory couldn't believe that he was doing all this for a chick. This wasn't like him at all, still something on the inside was telling him to stick with it.

## Chapter 35

Spence's friends threw him a bachelors party. They hired four strippers and invited about twenty friends. The strippers were the show but it was also a crowd of guys gambling playing tonk. Most of the guys there were working men, family men who came out to celebrate with their guy.

The strippers were twerking everywhere. The one on the pole had her foot all the way up leaning it on the pole like in a split with a corona bottle between her cheeks. The fellas went crazy over that. Cory made sure Spence stayed with some ass in his face. When he seen him go to the bathroom he sent a stripper in there after him.

Spence shut the door behind him and began taking a piss. Not soon after the door open and in came in one of the strippers. A little brown skin beauty who look like she was up to no good.

"I heard you needed help holding that thing," she said.

Spence chuckled, "You would do that for me? He do get heavy sometimes."

Cory had his ear to the door listening in. After hearing some moans and movements he went back and joined the party. He turned his focus on making sure he got laid for the night.

**\*\*\*\***

A few days later Cory found himself at another event with Asia thinking about how he couldn't believe he was about to go through with this all for a woman who still hadn't gave him any yet. He felt ashamed of himself but at the moment that feeling was dominated by nervousness. He was set up to be the guest speaker. It was for the kids but there were parents, staff, and other adults around also. This would be the first time he had ever given his spiel. The kids he was about to talk to were at risk kids because of their environment. Just coming out of the house they seen a lot so aint no telling what they had seen in their house.

Cory felt like he went over his speech a thousand times yet he still felt unprepared. He played it cool but when it was on him he struggled to find the words to start his speech off with. He knew he couldn't afford to choke though. Staring down into them kids eyes he felt sorry for them. He knew what they were up against. Their future, whatever they were experiencing in their young lives now was only the beginning of what the hood had in store for them. They gave him their undivided attention. Cory looked through the window to their souls and seen them yelling for help. At that moment he felt like only he could save them. The responsibility of that thought caused him to push his nervousness to the side and put on his cape. For the next half an hour he opened up to them, telling them about drugs, negative versus positive people, how he did time because he wanted to run the streets, and why education is important. He used himself and his experiences for examples of what not to do. Not only was the kids wowed but everyone there was also. Asia learned things about him that she wasn't able to get out of him with her usual questions. Everyone could tell that he was being genuine.

After he finished there was a Q and A session and the kids began opening up talking about their problems, something he wasn't expecting. They talked about bullying and peer pressure but the biggest issues was coming from their own homes. The fathers who weren't there and the mothers who spent more time going out and in the streets than they did nurturing a relationship with their kids.

The parents in the room listened attentively. They never got these kind of responses out of the kids. They were hearing things they never heard before, things the kids wasn't comfortable with telling them because they felt like they couldn't relate. Cory gave them his sincerest advice. Knowing that it might not be enough he only wished that he could have done more.

A burden had been lifted off of Cory as the session came to an end. He felt good, like he'd really made an impact. It was an invigorating feeling that he'd never felt before. He had been happy about certain things in the past but talking to them kids made him proud of himself. He was glad to have gone through with it.

"You did good," Asia said complimenting him.

"Thanks, it's sad what some of them kids are going through. I wish I could do more."

"You can if you really want. You can make a good living going around talking to kids, doing appearances at schools, centers, and other places. It's a need for guys that have been through what you've been through to help deter these kids from getting in trouble."

"How much are you talking," Cory asked interested?

"I don't know but I can find out. I also may can get you to speak at Lakeland Juvenile Center if you want. Them the kind of kids who really need it because they already getting in trouble. Some of them are already over their heads in the streets. They need guidance and someone who really cares."

Something about that day sparked a change in Cory. It was the first time he did something good and actually felt good about doing it without receiving any monetary gain. One night while talking Asia had told him that one out of every three black men will go to prison. Knowing that he was a part of that statistic made him want to be part of the solution rather than the problem.

\*\*\*\*

Asia and Ebony were waiting to get their dresses from the tailor. Everything in the wedding was going to be color coordinated, including what the guess was going to wear.

"Some of the things Cory shared with them kids were frightening. I was worried about how you was going to see him afterwards," Ebony told Asia on their way back to the car.

"It was intriguing. The thing is I don't think he really understands how deep some of the things are he was saying, because where we grew up them type of things are regular but not everyone goes through it. He held them kids attention the whole time and got them to open up at the end. All this time we been around them they haven't open up to us like that. The girls yeah, but not the boys."

"You're right," Ebony responded. "What did he think about it?"

"He said that he liked it." I'm going to try to get him to talk to the kids at Lakeland."

"That's going to be a tough one," Ebony said.

"Yeah, I know," replied Asia. "He's going to do good though, I believe in him. I told him that he has to talk to them different than he did the kids at our center. He said yeah yeah yeah, he got this playing around. You know how men are. I believe he got it though. Who else better than someone who was once one of them."

"Everything must be going well with ya'll you talking about you believe in him."

"It's alright, I'm still trying to hold out," Asia said laughing. "I'm scared to be alone with him, I might just give him the goodies."

"I bet he feel like you torturing him. He must really like you."

"I'm not trying to torture him. We haven't made it official yet."

"Ya'll are into one another, so what's the hold up?"

"I guess we're still getting to know one another."

What Asia talked to Ebony about was on her mind. She knew she had to stop playing the friendship game before some other women came and snatched Cory up from under her nose. It was no doubt that she wanted him but she wanted everything to be right. She was into the whole romance thing but Cory didn't seem like too much of a romantic guy. For the most part she led the way, but she believed that a man should work for it, value it, and approach it in the right manner, Not like an animal.

****

A week later Cory spoke at Lakeland. A spot full of hell raisers. Almost all of them locked up for drugs or violent crimes. All of them thinking that they're already grown, done seen it all and been through it all. Cory could tell that at first they weren't too beat. When he began talking he started talking their language and they were paying close attention. That's when he knew he had them. He told them about his old mindset, how he sold drugs and use to put work in. That's what captivated them because that's what they were into, the whole movie, the song of it all, but then he hit them with the flip side, the reality of things. He managed to do all that while keeping it interesting, entertaining, and relatable.

Cory was once their age. He did time in that same spot, he knew the mindset. He also knew that while they may have been feeling what he was saying at that moment that once they got back on them tiers they were going to run wild, forgetting everything he said. It was a sad truth however he kept Asia's words in mind. (Just maybe you could make a difference in one of their lives.) Life and experience are the best teachers. Most people learn from trial and error, so it was only right that they'll live and learn. Cory left there feeling like he connected with them kids in a major way.

## Chapter 36

Spence and Malia's wedding consisted of about two hundred people, all friends and family. Spence stood at the alter occasionally patting his forehead with his napkins to wipe away the little beads of sweat that kept popping up. He tried to wait patiently and proudly but Cory could see a little of uncertainty on his friend's face. A smirk flashed across Cory's face. He knew that the pressure was on Spence. He thought back to the old Eddie Murphy comedy show when Eddie was talking about how women be trying to take half of everything once dudes marry them. Spence had a nice six figure salary. Cory hoped that he had a prenuptial agreement.

"You must be thinking about some good stuff," Deron whispered to Cory. "Care to share?"

"I was in my own little world just now," Cory told Deron.

Here comes the bride began playing. A little girl came walking down the aisle sprinkling rose peddles. Malia's father walked her down the aisle ready to give her away. It was truly a beautiful site. Cory had never seen black love displayed so eloquently before. He listened to every word as they stood in front of one another reading off their vows. The love they claimed for one another was heart felt. He secretly wished he could love and be loved like that. Before witnessing these moments he only thought love like this existed in movies, now he was a true believer. His eyes became a little watery, he sniffled while wiping them. On hearing him sniffle Deron looked over at him with a smirk. He couldn't believe it. The only reason why he didn't say anything was because he didn't want to disturb Spence while he was reading his vows.

Cory felt him looking and knew that he had got caught slipping and that he'll end up hearing and getting laughed at later. He gave Deron a little nudge with his arm. No one else could see it because they were side by side. Afterwards Cory looked over to where Asia was seated and caught her looking at him. He wondered how long have she been watching him.

"I DO!" Spence and Malia started kissing. He picked her up and began spending around with her. They walked down the aisle happily married. Everyone clapped, threw rice, and let balloons go into the air.

The wedding was held under a big white tent set up with sheer drapes to keep the bugs out. It had two sections. One where the wedding took place, another where the party had just begun. The first thing Malia did was throw the bouquet back. All the ladies were jockeying for position trying to get it, including Asia and Ebony.

"Look at them beasting. They take that stuff seriously, don't they," Cory joked with the fellas.

"Every unmarried women here want that," Deron said.

"I bet ya lady get it," Cory joked. "Look at her face. She look like she about to start a royal ruble for that thing."

Deron looked at her and how serious she was and began laughing.

Malia threw a hell mary back over her head high in the air. Cory seen Asia in the crowd trying to get it. *What is she doing, she don't even have a man,* he thought to himself. They haven't even had sex yet so they were far from a ring. He wasn't worried, he been told himself that he wasn't ever going to get married.

Deron's lady was knocking women over, stepping on them, and throwing elbows trying to get the bouquet. She was in the best position to score but out of nowhere this chick came flying across everyone intercepting the bouquet in midair. She hit the ground without even bracing herself. Unfazed she got up happy holding the bouquet in the air dancing like she had just scored a touchdown.

"Dam, who was that" Cory asked in a joking tone.

"I don't know," Deron responded.

E.J. ran toward the crowd to help out the woman who looked like she had hit her head on the ground. Bout time he got there she was up bouncing up and down with the trophy hoisted up. With a big smile she jumped into E.J.'s arms giving him kisses all on his face.

"O shit, that's E.J.'s girl," Cory said laughing with the fellas. The other ladies who were competing walked off disappointed.

The cake was five stories high with little figures of Spence and Malia standing on it. Malia cut the first piece and fed it to Spence then took a bite of the same slice. She laughed as Spence chewed his food with some cake smeared on the side of his lips. She wiped it off then kissed that exact spot.

Moments later they had their first dance to the R-Kelly song (Step in the name of love). Everyone stood around, the next song everyone was on the floor having a good time. Cory and Asia were on the dance floor holding one another talking more than they were dancing. Her head was on his chest, his arms engulfed her.

"Cory, when are you going to ask me to be your woman?" Asia wasn't going to give herself to him without being in a committed relationship.

"I wasn't," he responded.

She took her head off of his chest and looked at him.

"I didn't know how," he said looking down at her. "I'm not use to this lovely dovey stuff."

"Well get use to the lovely dovey stuff," Asia joked causing Cory to laugh. "Go ahead and ask me."

Cory had been dwelling on this whole situation for a while now. He didn't know if he was quite ready for her, if she was too good for him or what but he knew that he liked her a lot. Enough to even think about settling down. He inhaled deeply and when he exhaled he spoke the words as softly and seductively as he could into her ear. "Asia would you like to be my woman?"

"I don't know, are you done with all your other female friends?"

"What female friends?"

"The ones that be calling you when we're together. You didn't think I thought they were all guys calling, did you?" You know I'm smarter than that."

"Yeah, I'm done with all that. I want you. I believe you're special. You have to promise me one thing though."

'Anything Cory."

"Promise that you won't break my heart."

Asia found it cute that he was worried about getting his heart broke. Usually it was the female who was worried about stuff like that.

"I'll never break your heart Cory. I'll love to be your woman."

They kissed. Now Cory was feeling like he had gotten married. After being shitted on by Keisha when he was locked up he told himself that he was done with relationships. He was only going to smash chicks, and not get into any of that emotional stuff. Now he found himself going against all of that. It was time to face the facts. He fell in love.

"Come on, let's go consummate this thing," Cory said playing pulling her.

"No stop," Asia said laughing. "Be patient, we got all night to make that happen."

For the rest of the night Asia was on his arm. There was a lot of single ladies there looking for men. Asia made it clear that the one she was with was no longer on the Market. The rest of the evening was spent dancing, socializing, sipping wine and meeting new people. Majority of the people there Cory didn't know but somehow through Spence he met most of them.

"These some good people I'm introducing you to," Spence said. "This is how you network bro. You never know what you could run into. That's why you have to stay open minded and positive. Look around, these are my colleagues and associates." Spence had his arm around Cory leaning on him a bit. He had been drinking so Cory knew that he was in his bag. He started pointing out different people. He's the CEO of this company, he owns that company, he's a partner at such and such firm, he was going on and on. Even introducing him to a couple of sports figures.

Cory was drained when him and Asia left. She drove, he sat back in the passenger seat trying not to pass out. They talked all the way to her house. Cory felt like tonight was the night. The energy was good, they had made their relationship official, and she seem to want him as bad as he wanted her. He was so drained that he was unsure if he was going to be able to perform to his potential but he definitely was going to try. He waited way too long not to.

Asia lived in Camden. She could have been left the hood but she loved her community. It was almost twelve O'clock on a Friday night. The night was still young, especially for what they were anticipating. Cory had no ideas of the dangers that lurked across the street. The dude Cory did his bid over manz Ru spotted him. It was him and another dude. They were always strapped so when they seen Cory slipping they was on go. The other dude didn't know Cory. When Cory had gotten locked up he was still on the porch, running around picking his nose. That was back then, he had matured into a whole beast.

Asia got out of the car, Cory sluggishly followed her. He was tipsy but he still was being a gentlemen by grabbing all her things. She made her way to the house. Once all her things were in hand he followed. The only thing on his mind was getting to the pussy he'd been desiring for so many months. With every drunken step he felt like he was getting closer and closer to it.

One thing about the past is that it's always on our ass, literally and figuratively. Time could heal some wombs but some things you can't prepare for that's why some people don't let beefs die.

Before going up the steps Cory sense a presence, then heard a noise. Bout time he turned around it was too late. About fifteen shots rang out. The first causing Asia to whip her body around. What she witnessed was beyond her worse nightmare. It was over in seconds. The two guys ran off. Asia uncovered her mouth to begin yelling, "Help, help me, someone call the police." She ran down the steps and fell to her knees holding him. His body was convulsing uncontrollably.

"Please don't die, come on baby. You're going to make it. Everything will be alright." She screamed for help again. A few neighbors were out there on their phones already talking to the police. Cory was fighting to keep his eyes open. Every time he blanked his eyes stayed closed a little longer. Until he decided that his eyes closed felt better than trying to hold them open. His last vision was him looking up at Asia. Tears running down her face, she was saying something he couldn't understand. He could feel her love. He only wished he had a chance to feel more of it.

****

A couple of hours later the hospital was packed with Cory's concerned friends. Spence wasn't worried about his honeymoon. They had already missed their flight. Him and Malia was supposed to disappear to the Island of Belize for the weekend.

Everyone was still wearing their tuxes and dresses. Deron paced the floor praying that his manz was still alive. Ebony held Asia as she wept. She was covered in blood, her dress was ruined. That didn't cross her mind. She just saw the love she found get shot up. Praying that he made it was the only thing on her mind.

Kimberly rubbed E.J.'s back as he sat there tearing, hands balled up, furious. They all knew and grew up with guys who was slain in the streets but this was too close to home. Cory was like their brother. They were the only family he had.

"Doc Doc, is there anything on Cory Allen yet," Deron asked startling the Doctor?

"Yes there is," the Doctor said looking at his clip board. "He's in critical but stable condition. The next few hours will determine a lot."

"Can we see him," Asia asked in a sad tone?"

"Not right now, he's unresponsive. Maybe when he becomes a little better but his condition is moment to moment.

Asia closed her eyes and dropped her head in prayer. Ebony wrapped her arm around her.

Deron began walking with the Doctor. "Doc, everything real, what's the likely hood of my brother surviving?"

"He's in bad condition but he's strong, and in good health so he has a chance. I just can't say."

Deron knew it was bad but he agreed with the Doctor that Cory was strong so he knew that the hope was there. "Alright, take care of him Doc."

"I will," the doctor said stepping off.

For the next couple of days Cory's friends practically lived in the waiting room. Ebony had to force Asia to go home and change her blood soiled clothes. It wasn't until Sunday that they were able to see Cory. He was hooked to a machine laying there in a coma. The nurse told them that he hasn't been woke since the surgeries. Asia tried to hold it together. She pulled a chair up to his bed side, everyone else was standing looking over him. They really didn't know what to say because he was sleep.

The next few days everyone went back to work except Asia. She faithfully sat by his side. Sometimes Ebony would go just to bring her friend something to eat and keep her company. She had never seen her like this over a man before. She basically shut down her daily activities to be there for Cory.

"Dear God," Asia prayed. With both of her hands she held his right hand against her forehead as she leaned on the side of the bed. "I try my best to live righteously. I know that might haven't been the case for Cory but I love this man like no other. I'm begging you god, please deliver him to me in good health and sound mind. Please don't let him die," she asked sobbing. Miraculously she felt his hand move. Her head popped up and she was surprised to see him looking down at her. God had answered her prayers.

"Cory you're woke," she said. She caressed his forehead before kissing it. "You're going to be alright baby, I'm going to make sure of it. Let me get the Doctor for you," she said before pushing the button.

The nurses had told Asia if he wake up to call her so that's what she did. One nurse came in checking his vitals and asking him questions. His mouth was dry and his voice was crackly. He kept trying to clear his throat to speak. He tried mumbling something but gave up because it wasn't coming out loud and clear.

Asia was elated that Cory had made so much progress. Once the nurse left Asia showed him how happy she was. She kept talking and expressing herself. Cory didn't have to say anything back. She just wanted him to feel her love and know that it was real.

The next day Asia was able to go to work knowing that Cory was getting better. After work she came right back to the hospital. While approaching the room she could tell that he had other visitors. Two dudes, one sounded irate. He was expressing himself loud enough for a little of everyone in the hospital to hear him.

"I got you brah, he done. Him and his dudes. It's war, fuck that," Pettie was saying when Asia walked up. He was unconscious of how loud he really was. He quieted up and step to the side when she came through.

"How you doing," he respectfully spoke.

"Hello," she said walking by him going to Cory's bed side. She put her handbag on the chair kissed Cory then asked, "how are you doing baby?" She intruded with a mentality that let Pettie know Cory didn't need to be hearing all that non-sense. It was healing time and only with good energy was that possibly. She despised the whole thug mentality because she knew it only led to black on black violence which was a result of her people being taught to hate each other so they'll never unit and be as powerful as they could really become. Another one of the man tricks.

Asia or Cory wasn't paying his friends any mind. Cory was now able to talk and move around a little. His energy changed when she came into the room. He went from laying down listening to his supposed to be friends talk negative about how they was going to revenge him to excitedly sitting up to give Asia a hug and kiss when she came through.

Pettie could sense that love was in the air. "Cory, I'm out bro. I'll keep you updated on that," he said before departing.

"Alright," Cory said never taking his eyes off of Asia. The fact that she didn't leave that hospital when he was in that coma spoke volumes. He could hear her voice and feel her love. He couldn't remember what she was saying but love is an expression that one only needs to feel to fully understand it.

"How you feeling?"

"Much better, that medicine be having me doped up."

"Well don't get addicted to it. That's how people get hooked on other things."

"I'm not going out like that," he said holding up his arm showing her his bicep. He grimaced putting his arm back down. He was hurting."

"Be careful. You're still healing." Asia began fixing the covers on him so he could stay warm. "Cory, that guy who was in here was talking crazy, I heard him all the way down the hall. I don't want you involved with anything that's going to get you in trouble."

"He wasn't really talking about anything," he said trying to downplay the whole ordeal but Asia wasn't stupid.

"I hope you're not trying to get revenge for this. I know how it is. Tell me you won't do anything stupid Cory."

Asia was serious. She wanted him to promise. He didn't want to lie to her so he tried to avoid talking about it but she wouldn't drop the subject.

"Asia, look at me. Mothafuckas tried to kill me. I'm sitting here pissing and shitting out of tubes. Somebody gotta feel it, fuck that! I know I aint in the streets no more but I still can't let dudes think they can get away with this. I can't be the victim. Next time I might not be so lucky."

Asia let him vent. She never heard him curse like that before. He usually tried to keep it clean around her. The situation had him heated though. That fact that he was trying to be on some square stuff and something like this still happened to him had him about to give up. That I don't give fuck attitude was always right there and if it wasn't for the good people he had in his life he would have embraced it. Guys like Pettie fed them demons when he came around talking about revenge. Asia knew this. She didn't know Cory or how he used to be but she knew that hanging with the wrong crowd wouldn't bring him any good.

"You have to understand Asia, I'm just a hood dude trying to stay out of trouble and get ma shit together. But none of this square shit feel right. It feel like I'm going against my nature."

Asia stood up with tears in her eyes. Cory reached out taking her hand and brought her closer.

"I'm sorry Asia, it's the way things are." She sat in the edge of the bed and he pulled her in hugging her.

"It don't have to be like that Cory. I don't want to lose you," she said as they hugged each other.

"I don't want to lose you either."

****

Over the next few days many visitors had went to see Cory. The one person who was there every day was Asia. Deron and E.J. came when they could. Asia had talked to them about talking Cory out of trying to get revenge. Kim had accompanied E.J. on one hospital visit. Ebony would bring her loyal friend some food every couple of days. ED, Cory's boss from the gym had come up there once talking like he wanted to get somebody whacked. Asia wasn't there to hear any of that, but she did happen to be there when Jenny showed up.

Cory painfully sat up when he seen Jenny. He and Asia was sitting there talking. The last thing he needed in his life right now was relationship drama.

Not paying Asia any mind the first thing Jenny did was give Cory a hug. "O my god, I'm so happy you're okay," she said.

Asia was feeling some type away about another woman hugging her man but she wasn't ignorant. She wanted to see how they interacted. That would give her all the information she needed. She definitely wanted to know who this woman was. The hug was awkward for Cory. He quickly introduced them, letting Jenny know that Asia was his lady. Jenny got the message, they had been creeping around her relationship for months. She barely stayed for ten minutes before wishing them both well then departing.

Jenny wasn't the only one who went to visit him. Eve and Chantel visited at different times. Both were loud and dramatic. They didn't show Asia any respect. They were hugging Cory, sticking their butts out all extra knowing Asia was right behind them. Cory introduced Asia as his lady but that didn't seem to make a difference. Both times Asia bit her tongue. She wasn't with the drama. This gave her a chance to see exactly the kind of women Cory was used to. She wasn't impressed at all.

Eve came through second, on a different day than Chantel. Once Asia seen how ignorant she was she exited early. She didn't see it as a trust issues with having her around her man. If Cory was going to choose Eve over her then she felt that's the kind of women he deserved.

As soon as Asia left Eve started telling Cory how she wanted him back. Cory wasn't beat, he kept trying to curve the conversation. He was glad when she finally left. He spent the rest of the night thinking about Asia. The difference between her and the women he dealt with was evident, like night and day. He kept thinking about how much of an amazing woman Asia was. The things she did for him, how she was there, and how he didn't want to lose her. *Sometimes you have to recognized when you're blessed. It's hard to find love and loyalty,* he thought to *himself.* Without her he would have had a lot of lonely nights in that hospital.

## Chapter 37

When it was time for Cory to learn how to walk again Asia was right there making sure he was good. She took off of work and her community activities to be by his side. The nurses only did the minimum.

Thoughts about how not any female would have been there for him like that increased his feelings for Asia. The females he was accustomed to dealing with would have been using that free time to cheat with their other dudes. Cory knew and respected the game mainly because he didn't care about them. He didn't deal with emotions which was why he was able to play and not feel any type of way.

All that stuff Eve and Chantel was talking about how they missed Cory, loved him, wanted to be with him, and how they were going to start coming up there every day was just words. They never came back after that day. He didn't miss them not one bit. He had Asia, she was passing every test without him having to really test her. He stayed up all night watching T.V. thinking about her.

The next day Cory woke up to the beautiful site of Asia standing by his bed side taking off her jacket. His eyes popped open and he sat up excited. The therapy and rehab had Cory feeling better. He was now able to get out of bed and move around.

Asia expressed how she felt about the women who had came there to visit him while she was there. Cory told her how before they were together he did have other women in his life. He apologized and let her know that it really wasn't anything and that he'll shut all that down. That was a quick remedy to let her know that he wanted her not them.

"Those are the kind of women you're into," Asia asked making a disgusted face?

Cory couldn't do anything but shake his head. He knew she was talking about Eve and Chantel. They came in there acting like Shanaynay and Keylowlow from The Martin Lawrence show. The whole time he was embarrassed.

"I don't know what I was thinking. All I know is that I have a new acquired taste only for Asia."

She smiled, he brought her in close and they began kissing. "See what you did," Cory said showing her that he was hard.

"You silly," she said after looking down.

"Go ahead and touch it."

He was poking through the hospital gown. Asia didn't mind being naughty for her man. She softly grabbed it and leaned against him and they began kissing.

"You know we can get a quickie in, right?"

"A quickie aint going to do it for me. I need this thing all night," she said still gripping his manhood. "Don't worry, it's going to be worth the wait. A hospital isn't my style."

Cory had to respect that. He settled for the lovely dovey kissing and holding, but he couldn't wait to get some for real.

****

The time in the hospital gave Cory and Asia time to enjoy each other mentally. They had gotten to know each other's past and was building on their future. They made plans to move in together. Cory only agreed if the house wasn't in the city. Asia had found a house in Deptford. A place still close enough for her to commute to work every day without a problem.

The same day he left the hospital they went to go see the house. She wanted him to approve of it but whatever she had picked out that's what he was going with. He just wanted to feel safe. The other house he had he was going to rent out.

The moving company took a day to move everything from both of their houses to the new one. Afterwards they stood side by side looking at all the boxes.

"Where do we get started," Asia asked?

"How about we save this for another time and go out," Cory suggested.

"Where to?"

"Let's go get something to eat. In fact, let's go to that poetry spot you took me to before. We could eat and enjoy some good old poetry."

"You trying to impress me?"

"If I was you wouldn't mind."

"You right," Asia said smiling nodding her head. "I can go for something that's going to soothe my soul right now. Shall we get dressed?"

"Not today. We aint trying to impress anybody, we already got each other," Cory said wrapping his arms around her hips and bringing her in for a soft kiss.

Warm Daddy's had a mellow vibe. The relaxed ambience of the lounge was popular with couples and people who were out on dates. The food as well as the entertainment was good. Often if one didn't have a table reserved they would have to wait for one to open up. This day Asia and Cory was able to get a table without the wait. They had some drinks while waiting for their food. They chatted and enjoyed the entertainment. Asia was talking about this trip they were about to go on with the kids.

Cory sat across from her mesmerized thinking about how she was such a beautiful soul. A woman with a purpose, goals, a vision, who was committed to something bigger than herself was a turn on. Their conversations flowed effortlessly. Cory always did most of the question asking because he always wanted to know more. Their bond was like putting a missing piece of the puzzle together that fitted perfectly. He enjoyed a since of peace around her.

Cory had the Catfish, jerk wings, hot wings and firecracker shrimp with sauces for dip. Asia had the Bar-B-Q Atlantic Salmon with a Country Caesar Salad. She nibbled on his and her own plates while Cory ate like he was trying to get the weight back that he lost while he was in the hospital.

The food was done but he wasn't. The Patron had him feeling nice. "I'll be back," Cory said. Asia's eyes followed him as he staggered off. He walked up to some guy said a couple of words and turned around walking pass her again to the stage. Them being there wasn't a coincidence, it was a part of Cory's surprise.

Cory walked up to the microphone and began adjusting it to his level. Asia began smiling, it finally occurred to her that he was going to try to recite a poem. It was funny because she knew that he didn't know much about poetry but she admired him for having the courage to go up there. Now she wanted to hear how it was going to turn out.

Cory stood up there unexpectedly confident for someone who was about to recite a poem in front of all these people for the first time. Secretly he had been working on poems while in the hospital. All of them inspired by Asia. This one he was about to recite was dear to him. He knew for a fact she would love it. Like the amateur he was he pulled a piece of paper out of his pocket. After unfolding it he cleared his throat and begun.

You suddenly came through and instantly changed the game,

With your beauty, intelligence, kindness and perfect body frame,

You're a perfect picture without paint, forced the devil to become a saint,

Being wit you I can be myself without any restraints,

Falling in love and giving my heart to a woman goes against my beliefs,

You robbed me for my love and stole my heart like a thief,

I love, respect, honor and adore you for being my peace,

I used to think love was overrated,

Since you came into my life that thought is now faded,

you're a great joy into my life, you're truly loved and appreciated.

Asia listened attentively to every word. She was not only surprised at how good the poem was, but she was also touch by the things he said about her. He wasn't the best at expressing himself so she had no ideal he felt that way. He said things in that poem that he didn't say to her directly and for everyone else in there to hear it was flattering. He received a standing ovation when he was finished. The women kept their eyes on him as he walked off stage. They wanted to see who the lucky lady was.

There was a weight lifted off of Cory's shoulders. He felt like he had did it. He walked off stage with an innocent smile waving at everyone as they clapped for him. When he came over Asia gave him a warm hug and kiss, there was no words spoken. Cory's next move wasn't a part of the plan. It was so spontaneous that it even shocked him. He knelt down in front of her holding her hand. Asia took a deep breath and covered her mouth. She was speechless. All the other women there were watching, they started standing up and coming closer. The music had stopped, the spotlight was on them. Cory began spilling his heart out.

"Asia, you're probably the most beautiful person I know. Not just your looks, you have a heart of gold. The qualities you possess is all that I ever wanted in a woman and more. You taught me how to love again. Words can't express how special you are to me. I'm blessed to have you as my woman. I really would love for you to be my wife though. I don't have a ring right now but I promise if you'll be my wife I'll work doubles every day of my life to get you the most beautiful ring you ever seen."

By now Asia had tears in her eyes. "Yes yes," she said hugging him.

They both only had one thing on their minds when they got home that night. They didn't bother to open them boxes, fix anything or even put the sheets on their bed. As soon as they walked in the door they excitedly began stripping off each other's clothes. Cory had been waiting for this moment for way too long. He didn't know if he was going to beat the box up or take his time with it. He figured he'll figure it out, at the moment he was just trying to get in it.

Once they made It upstairs Asia came out of her clothes revealing a stunning chocolate figure. Cory was all over her. His hands caressing all of her soft spots. Their tongues tangled as he laid her on the bed. She opened her legs ready to receive him. He got on top of her and began kissing on her neck, and ear then made his way to her breast. He wanted to make sure she was really ready for him before he entered her fortress. He took his time caressing and kissing her body. Massaging her clitoris, then taking the juices from her pussy and rubbing them on her clitoris. Eyes closed, head to the side, biting her bottom lip Asia moaned through the sensation. Her legs were wide open. She was grabbing at him so he could stop playing and come get some.

He finally connected his body to hers. The moans became noises. He could feel her walls caving in on him as he slid in deeper and deeper. Then she put her hand on his stomach. A man didn't have to be a football playa to hate this type of stiff arm. That was the least of his worries though. A few strokes and her arms were wrapped around his back.

What he couldn't believe was how good the pussy was. He was only about twenty strokes in and felt like he was about to come already. He tried fighting it but that was always a hard one, especially while he was still humping away. His mind played ping pong with thoughts of either pulling out and waiting until his nut went down or just letting it all blow. Still tender from not having sex in months he let it blow. Afterwards he rolled over and sighed.

Asia sensed the disappointment and began kissing him on the cheek.

"I was too excited. I'ma reenergize in a minute," he guiltily admitted.

"Don't worry baby, I got this," Asia said planting wet kissing on his neck. She went down giving him more than he expected. How good her suck game was surprised him. She took her time and finessed his piece the right way reviving it instantly. Then hopped on top and began riding him. Another surprise, she did everything so well. Her sex game was nasty yet elegant. Consistent in her motion, making sure everything went in and out. The way she moved her hips, the faces and noises she made only added to the romance and showed how much she was really into it.

Her noises got louder as she started going harder. She was coming and Cory knew it. They both was going hard, he wanted to take her there. He grabbed the back of her neck and squeezed it and reached his other hand around to rub her butt hole. He got that wet with her pussy juices and in a circular motion applied the right amount of pressure. Not trying to insert his finger though. She was going crazy. He bit her cheek. As she was about to come he could feel her walls contracting. That had him on the edge. When she started coming it was like the levees breaking. Her juices came gushing back to back all over him. She kept having orgasms.

Cory wanted to switch positions. His stomach was extra wet when he got up. He was about to come and he wanted to finish off hitting it from the back. She put her face in the pillow, stretched her torso out and tutted her butt up just how he liked it. Her pussy was soak and wet when he rubbed it. He wiped the wetness on her butt and started hitting it.

Watching himself go in and out Cory slow stroked. The view from the back was amazing. He was taking it all in, appreciating every piece of her body. The intentions was to make love to her all night, but the dog in him began taking over. Her pussy was too good. His second nut was coming way sooner than expected. He grabbed a handful of her hair and started going harder. She stuck her face in the pillow to muffle her cries. He went harder and harder until he was there then he just buckled. Asia flattened out and he stayed stuck to her. They just laid there cuddled up.

■■■■■■■■■■■■■■■■■■■■■■■■■■■■■■■■■■■■■■■■■■■■■■■■■■■■■■■■■i

## Acknowledgements

Special thanks to my mother Neptina McNeal, family, Sheena, anyone who has ever supported me in any type of way, who has ever encouraged me along the way or who has respected me striving in the right way. Hopefully, you will continue to ride with me throughout this journey as I continue to show my creativity and produce.

Special thanks to my cover designer: @imAmalKunar, and @s.jewel_dropper for the poem by Cory.

Print name:

Address:

City:                    State:                    Zip:

Phone:


Mail to: Parkside Entertainment LLC

P.O. Box 2176

Clementon, NJ 08021

Parksideentertainmentllc.com

Instagram: @Tyemease @ParksideEntertainment

Facebook:  TyeMease

| Name | Quantity | Date | Price |
|---|---|---|---|
| Poetic Kisses | | | |
| Gucci Girls | | | |